BRAVING THE ELEMENTS

Darkness Series # 2

K.F. BREENE

Hazy Dawn Press, Inc.

BRAVING THE ELEMENTS

Sasha has always known she was different, but now she also knows that the shadow men she's seen all her life, are real.

With a life goal of fitting in, Sasha hopes her strange abilities will finally make true friendship a possibility. Unfortunately, her magic doesn't function like everyone else's. What she thought would make her belong, sets her apart now more than ever.

Stefan, all but promised to a different woman, has tried to keep his mind on his duties instead of the irresistible and free-spirited human. But when she is threatened, he can't keep his distance anymore. He'll stop at nothing to keep her safe, and more importantly, make her his.

Just when one thing clicks into place, another spirals out of control. Stefan's clan isn't the only group that would benefit from an extremely rare type of magic. And their enemies will stop at nothing to get what they want.

Want to stay in the loop?
Sign up to be the FIRST to learn about new releases. Plus get newsletter only bonus content for FREE. Click here to sign up.

CHAPTER ONE

My alarm clock was a flick to the head.

"Ow!" I rubbed the offending spot as I opened my bleary eyes.

Charles, my once jovial and immature sidekick, would, starting this evening, become my grumpy and brooding fellow student. I had been warned of this several times in the last two weeks as I got used to my new home in Stefan's mansion. With a bunch of vampire-resembling people.

"I'm a light sleeper, all you have to do is tell me to wake up," I said in a matching grump, climbing out of the bed, which just felt wrong at five o'clock in the evening.

"Not as gratifying. C'mon, we have to go."

Wiping my puffy eyes, I groaned. Charles's kind was largely nocturnal, sleeping all day and active at night. They didn't have a phobia of the sun, they just preferred the night —the reverse of humans. And because it was the reverse of humans, I'd found this new schedule—one I had tried to acclimate to over the past fourteen days—grueling. I wasn't sleeping well during the daylight hours, and had a hard time keeping my eyes open near midnight and beyond, especially because I was using the time to work with knives and run obstacle courses to try and get in shape. It was a rough start to my new life.

But hopefully soon it would be different. I started instruction tonight to learn my craft—which was apparently magical in nature. How cool was that? So far I had done weird things while in the throes of danger, but now I would hopefully learn how to do weird things whenever I wanted!

Not only that, but I would get to make friends without worrying about that part of me that was always different from everyone else. The part that saw human-shaped shadows lurking in the night and had a sixth sense about pop quizzes or someone's intentions. Since the shadow-people had turned out to be real and not some mental disorder, and my intuition could probably be explained with magic, I no longer had to hide. I could just be me, with the possibility of real intimacy and lasting friendships—something I'd always been denied until now. I would finally fit in!

I squeaked in excitement.

Charles answered with a glower. "You're excited for nothing. This is gonna suck."

"Oh, relax. It'll be fun."

The glower intensified.

I did sympathize with him. I would be seriously pissed if I had to go back to high school. Or college for that matter. Charles had been through all this magic stuff before. He was a big shot in Stefan's band of warriors even though he was really young for the position. But now he had to guard me, in case their enemy came after me, and go through school all over again because Stefan thought he'd benefit from it. Charles was not enthused, but I got the feeling no one said 'no' to Stefan.

My stomach filled with butterflies. Just thinking of Stefan had my heart leaping. Since the first time I'd laid eyes on him,

I'd been hooked. Uncommonly handsome with a lethal grace, Stefan could melt my body with a look. In the last two weeks, as I wandered around the mansion trying to learn about my new residence, I'd seen him from a distance. He'd be crossing the hall or exiting the house, busy and important with people leaning on his every word. He ran this establishment and everyone in it. He'd always look my way, without fail, seeming to feel my presence as I always felt his. His eyes would linger on my face, and then sweep my body, before his brow crumbled in something like guilt. His stare always turned frustrated and hostile right before he looked, and walked, away.

Charles assured me it was just because he was busy. That he was always like that. I really hoped so. I wanted to fit in here. Also...I had a weird attachment to him. Attraction bordering on distraction—whenever he was near; it was like my heart reached out to join his. When he wasn't around, I constantly thought about him, wanting to be closer. I'd never felt anything like it. It was like a sweet addiction I never wanted to give up; but at the same time, needing someone that much scared the pants off me. It was a dicey situation.

I wiped my mind clear and followed Charles out of my secret hideaway at the edge of the huge property. It was a small house with a crap-load of spells, chants, incantations, and what not. Basically, it was invisible unless you knew it was there and stared really hard. Or, if the sun or moonlight hit it just right. Only three people could gain entry without some sort of alarm going off—me, Charles and apparently Stefan, though Stefan had never come to visit.

I suddenly felt like kicking something.

"What class is first on the agenda?" I asked, nearing the back entrance of the busy mansion. Tall and graceful people sauntered about their business, mostly attractive and all slightly sensuous. These people had an extremely loose view of sexual relations, which was putting it mildly.

"We only have one for a few months. Elements. The most basic freaking class of magic workers. And I have to be seen taking it again like some flunky." Charles released a noisy breath and steered me to the left.

I patted his meaty shoulder. "Yes, but what would I do without you? You aren't a flunky, you are an important and necessary element to a human fitting in. You're like, the top of your class because you were chosen. Right?"

"Think you're awfully important, don't you…" Charles answered dryly. I could see the quirk of his lips, though. The pep talk seemed to help a little.

As we entered a dimly-lit hallway, my shoulder blades tingled from the stares. This had been happening since I started living here. People glanced at me because I was short and different, and then did a double-take, their eyes either stalling in confusion, suspicion, or like I had a ghost sitting on my shoulder rattling chains.

"Are you sure they're staring because I'm human?" I asked in a hush as a heavy, unyielding hand steered me around a corner. "Because I've occasionally seen a human or two—even though they were all dazed out by pheromones—and no one stared at them."

"You're different than them. You're unbalanced in the head."

"Why are you so grumpy? So you have to learn about these elements again, so what? You're still getting paid."

"Sasha, I like to kill stuff. I like to stab things with my sword. And yes, you can take that with a double meaning. If I'm sitting in a stuffy classroom, I can't do what I like. You could at least rectify *one* of those problems, but you refuse since you're a prude. Where exactly does that leave me?"

"I didn't know you knew words like 'rectify'…"

His eyebrows crawled down his nose as the corners of his mouth curled upwards. He wanted to hate me at the moment, but he did love to banter. Conundrum. "I might start beating you to take the edge off."

I snickered as we climbed the stairs and turned right. Then another right. Then a left. The place was *massive!* Eventually we strolled through an area that housed people who apparently didn't keep normal business hours.

"I feel like an ant in here." My gaze took in more than one naked person. "An overdressed ant."

"Well, you look like a jackass."

I rolled my eyes in Charles's general direction.

"Oh, Charles!" A man wearing a hat and a boner stopped us. "Is this your new pet? She is simply *divine!* Might I borrow her?"

"She bites sensitive areas," Charles replied in a dry tone as he steered me around the man and down the wide corridor.

"A red ant, then," I amended.

We scaled a grand staircase to the third floor and took a right.

"In you go." Charles opened the door and shoved me in front of him. I'd never seen him in such a bad mood.

After a second, I knew why.

A crowd of teens stood in the middle of a ballroom—all turned toward me, gawking. All different shapes and sizes, like human adolescents, they awkwardly stood, still growing into their bodies.

"They're all kids!" I exclaimed to Charles in a frantic whisper. "Isn't there a class my own age?"

"They are your age."

My gaze swept the room again. Baby fat in plenty, the girls stooped awkwardly, often taller than their male counterpart. The boys bounced and jostled each other, a few steps behind in maturity and none the wiser. They were definitely going through puberty, one and all.

I had lived on the other side of puberty for a great many years. These kids were not my age. I said as much.

"They've had the same number of trips around the sun, then. We just age differently. We live way longer. They're basically considered adults now, since their magic is coming in."

"They're still kids, though, Charles. Are there any other classes?"

"Magic hits at puberty, even in humans, though you seem too dimwitted to realize it—"

I elbowed him in the side. My arm bounced off muscle.

"I'm twenty-two, Charles. *Way* past puberty..."

"These children are here to develop their magic. I have already developed my magic. You have not. You belong here. I do not. I blame you for this."

"You burnt my house down! You owe me one."

His bushy eyebrows made a shelf over his eyes and his bottom lip protruded slightly. "Touché."

Point in my column.

"Hello, hello!" A man with a tall red hat and a cheery disposition strolled into the room. His smile would've been twinkling if this had been T.V. "Welcome everyone! I am your instructor, Master Hilbert. You can call me Master Bert. I will be helping you develop that very special little gift inside each and every one of you. Do you know what that gift is called? Mmm?"

"Magic!" an enthused student in the front row yelled.

"Maw, why yes! Good for you. Magic!"

"What does 'maw' mean?" I whispered.

"I think that's just a weird sound he makes," Charles answered just as quietly.

"First, let's get in a circle so we can see each other and introduce ourselves to the new pupils," Master Bert enthused.

While all the kids stood about my height, still growing, Charles topped the crowd and then some. The strongest and brawniest fighters with high power levels found themselves in the upper ranks of Stefan's army. It meant that Charles stood out a little. The young girls noticed.

"They're giggling!" Charles seethed.

"Yes, but just so you know, they are giggling *at* you, not *with* you."

"Shut up."

"Soon they will be laughing at you, not—"

"Shut up, I said."

I smirked, realizing I hadn't been listening to any of the names, and now Master Bert stared at me expectantly, a supportive smile on his face.

"I'm Sasha."

"Maw, yes! And you are a human, is that correct?"

A few girls gasped. A few boys' eyes sparked, and then roamed down my body.

Uncomfortably, I said, "Yes."

"Maw, yes! That is wonderful. I have trained humans before, so don't you worry. Now, who is this big, strong male next to you?"

"Charles. I'm a Watch Captain. Here to monitor my charge." He jerked his head in my direction.

"Wonderful, yes." Master Bert's gaze slid down Charles' body, noticing each bump and groove, stopping at his crotch.

In human-land, this teacher would get fired for that kind of behavior. But here in crazy-land, he got an erection and Charles preened at the notice. Good Lord.

"Alrighty. Elements. How exciting!" Master Bert rounded the room, eyeing each student. "Some of you are closer to harnessing your magic than others. Some will work with the elements immediately, and some will slide into it slowly." His eyes touched me and then moved on. "Maw, we are not here to race, we are here to stroll."

A couple students puffed up with a smug grin—over-achievers. I could spot one immediately.

"Is it possible to cheat in this class?" I whispered out the side of my mouth. I was terrible at school and great at survival. I wasn't proud of how I got by, but I did get by.

Judging by Charles's scoff, he didn't think cheating was necessary. *Although, he's not a valedictorian, either, so who is he to judge?*

"Now, let's talk elements, shall we?" Master Bert fluttered around happily. "Maw, as we know, we need to *receive* the elements. We need to open up, spread our arms wide, and pull from the very fiber of nature. Maw, yes, what a treat!"

My mind slipped sideways, like it always did when teachers started to drone on about important information. I tried to rein it back in, forcing myself not to care about the ballet bar against the wall...

I'll bet the padded walls actually covered mirrors, though. *I wonder if they have ballet lessons. I'd love to dabble with a shuffle ball change or two. Wait, is that ballet or tap...?*

The nudge nearly had me sprawled on the floor.

"Pay attention!" Charles whisper-yelled at me.

I scowled at him, rubbing my arm where an elbow-sized bruise was sure to crop up.

"Maw, so let's give it a try, shall we?" Master Bert waved everyone on, the rest of the class scrunching their faces in concentration.

"What are we trying?" I asked quietly.

"He talked for, like, two minutes. You can't pay attention for two minutes?"

My heart sank. Because no, I couldn't. Learning magic turned out to be no different than math or social sciences—I just couldn't retain information when it was lectured at me. I tried to pay attention, and soak it all up, but my focus just wouldn't stay put. Before I knew it, I'd been staring at a butterfly and thinking about random goings-on.

It had always been like this. In the past, I'd been so scared about all my secret box items, I didn't want to tell my foster parents that I might have a learning problem. Through high school, I'd always had Jared to help me manage.

Tears clouded my vision as I once again felt the loss of my ex-boyfriend. He was in Florida in a job Stefan hooked him up with on the sly. I'd wanted to be mad that Stefan was reorganizing my life without my say-so, but in this instance, I couldn't. Jared was doing extremely well, making a lot of money and approved for a loan to buy a house. Without me to drag him down, he was rising like bubbles in champagne.

But now I had no safety blanket and no tutor. Just a brooding giant pissed off that he had to learn elements with a girl who couldn't even pay attention long enough to learn names.

"Sorry," I muttered, lowering my face. I took a breath through a constricted chest and tried to feel for elements. Opening my mind, and feeling that heat in my chest, got me a firm feeling of expectation. But nothing happened.

"So?" Charles asked, trying to bend down to get a peek at my expression.

"Very good, Salline! You've pulled water. Maw, congrats!" Master Bert clapped for Salline, a beaming girl owning her overachiever status.

I took a deep breath. I could do this. I'd done it before. Somehow.

I closed my eyes and *focused*. Blackness greeted me, like I was meditating. I mentally searched, feeling for fire. I wiggled my toes, thinking of dirt. Air was easy—it was everywhere. I strained with it, trying to suck at air somehow.

"It is okay not to touch the elements on your first few

tries," Master Bert reiterated, but then quickly followed with, "Oh Marc, fabulous! Great work. And James—great!"

"You don't have to hold your breath to wrangle an element," Charles said with amusement.

Desperately, I strained harder, *searching*. I needed to be good at this! Without this, I had nothing. No job, no place to live, no friends—

Panicking, trying to turn my misting eyes away from Charles, who was grinning at me in mockery like he thought I was joking with him, I tried to *pull*. Except, I didn't know what I was pulling at or with. I tried to focus on the heat in my chest, which usually meant magic; but it just sat there, like a lump. I scratched my palms against my jeans—a nervous habit I did when I was staring down at a test filled with foreign information. It was a telltale sign of failure.

A light hand pressed my shoulder gently. Master Bert wore a kind expression. "It's okay—it often takes humans much longer to access their magic. Maw, some are never able to—it is cultural conditioning, not a personal matter. You should not take it personally."

A glance told me that every other person—every single one—was smiling in jubilation. Salline had a pale purple flicker in her palm.

Oh goodie, I'm the dummy in a class full of achievers. Something new and different for me...

Sarcasm wasn't helping.

Fear and the common feeling of failure welled up inside me. I shrugged at my stupid brain, the act practiced.

"Fantastic, class, fantastic!" Master Bert applauded. "Now, let's talk some theory, and then we'll try it again."

The rest of the lesson passed in a haze of foreign informa- tion, elbows from an increasingly solemn Charles (who had realized I wasn't joking), and another practice session containing everyone else's accomplishments.

"What's wrong?" Charles asked quietly when the class finally came to a close. "Usually you're all peppy and excited. Why'd you stop trying?"

I shrugged, slowing so a couple boys could file in front. "I just don't get it. I don't know what I'm doing."

"So? Since when do you give up?"

I shrugged again as we waited to get through the door, the usual traffic jam of everyone in a hurry to get out after class was no different here than anywhere else.

A boy in front of us pushed his friend. "You were the *last one*. What an idiot!"

"Shut up," the other boy spat. "I wasn't raised with an older brother like you were—how could I've known how? And besides, the human didn't get it at all."

"The human doesn't count. And hardly anyone has an older brother. Idiot!"

"Shut the hell up or I'm going to shove my foot up your ass!"

The first boy laughed harder, taunting. They would've gotten in a fight right there if not for Charles grabbing each by their shirts and tossing one first, and then the other, out the door. Limbs went flying.

"Don't worry about them, Sasha," Charles said in a low tone for my ears alone. "We know you can do it. You're just new to all this. You'll figure it out."

I shrugged.

"Stop shrugging and have some faith in yourself."

Jared said that to me all the time. Have faith in myself. I'd always commented that it was his job. And he always had. Except now, he was gone.

We hit the first floor. I paused, feeling that familiar tug from the back of the house. Where we should be headed for dinner, or to just go to bed. A glance told me the weird connection to Stefan was right—he stood in the center of the wide hallway, his body pointed directly at me, his eyes boring into mine. Like Moses parting the seas, people gave him a wide berth, his advisors standing by like a swat team on steroids.

He probably wanted to check up on his investment; find out what saving my life had yielded.

Goose egg, that's what.

Pity party. Who brought the confetti?

"Can you beguile cops into deciding they shouldn't hand out tickets for going outrageously fast?" I asked Charles, not really caring if he could or not.

"Uh...maybe we should head toward the Boss. He seems... I think he wants you to go to him. See how your first class went..."

"My, my, Charles. I had no idea your analytical skills could deduce the obvious. Well done."

"I don't like this defiance thing you got going with him. Someone's going to get hurt, and it's probably going to be me."

"I thought you wanted a little excitement."

"Excitement, Sasha. I didn't say public execution."

Stefan kept staring, the pull on my chest trying to drag my body toward him. And there was absolutely nothing in the entire world I wanted more than to let him fold me in his arms and make everything all right; to smooth all this away. But I would just be the human who got special treatment from the Boss—assuming he'd even leave his drop-dead gorgeous girlfriend and play nursemaid to a pain in the ass. His help would look like a hand-out if he stooped low enough to give it.

Jesus. Forget a pity party, I was throwing myself a pity bonanza.

"I'm going to get in my car and drive really, really fast. As in danger-ville fast. Can you keep the cops from hauling me to jail?"

"Yeah," he whined, staring at Stefan.

"Then let's go for a ride. Speed always makes me feel better."

A half hour later, the car was screaming down a two-lane road in the wooded area outside the city. Trees flashed by, a blur of shimmering green as the first rays of the sun sprinkled their leaves. I had to admit, I was partially testing Charles' resolve, trying to see if he could hack it without the jitters. I took turns like the car was on rails, using both lanes of the road when the car got a little squirrely—which was often—dodging other cars when there were any. He'd screamed like a little girl, twice.

"Oooohhhhhh sssshiiiiittt!" Charles clutched the dashboard as my Firebird pitched over the crest of a hill. Tires left the ground for a beat before crashing back down, and jousting us forward.

A manic grin spread over my face. I needed this.

"We should...oh shit...we should...*slow down*!" Charles braced for a turn, grabbing the handle on his door with a white-knuckled grip.

"C'mon, Charles, I'm not going that fast. I thought you were a tough Watch Captain."

"I can face my enemies head on with a sword," Charles said through clenched teeth. "I have no control over dying right now, Sasha. *Watch out for that tree!*"

The car squealed around the turn, drifting to the other side of the road. Where another car was waiting.

Oh crap!

A punch of adrenaline rocked my body. I let off the gas, easing the car back toward my side of the road as a horn blared. I tucked the wheels back beyond the yellow line as the crawling sensation of a close call permeated my limbs. Warmth took its place, hot and spicy, ready for action.

I let out a huge, silent breath and let the speed dwindle. Not today. I was exhausted.

"Done now?" Charles asked through a tight throat. "Can we go home?"

"Yeah, I think I'm good. That helped."

"What's the deal with needing an adrenaline rush?" Charles asked as we headed back. "How can it possibly help anything?"

I shrugged, the warmth in my chest still zinging through my body, smoothing out my nerves. "It thrills me somehow, which then seems to just calm everything down. I get a big high, and then just, kinda...level out. I don't know."

Charles squinted. "I bet the thrill wakes up the magic, and then it fills you. That's why you think you level out. You've probably learned to use your magic with that intuition thing you've talked about. You didn't have teaching so you learned a rough version of controlling it on your own."

"Quit analyzing me. My crazy needs no definition."

A frown joined the thinking squint. "When you try to reach for the magic, nothing comes. When you sprint at death, you apparently access it easily and then save the day. As the mastermind behind this operation, I find it my duty to figure this out."

"You figuring something out—yeah, that's going to happen...."

Charles sighed and shook his head. "Sarcasm. How helpful."

T he next day went the same. And, so did the day after. I just couldn't grab those danged elements. I didn't even know where to look! I was supposed to open up somehow, see them pulsing out there (no one would identify where *there* was), and pull them to me. What kind of cockamamie directions were those, anyway? Yeah, sure, just open on up and pull at some imaginary, universal power streams. Good call. I'll just do that, shall I?

It made no sense.

Each day after class, Stefan would be waiting in a place where I was sure to run into him. The weird link I had with him, which seemed to have gotten stronger since the last time he saved my life, hinted that he was worried. About me? About his clan? I didn't know; but yesterday, when I finally wanted to give in and sob in defeat on his chest, that tart, Darla, had been loitering around, giving me eye-threats. No way did I want to mess with her. Plus, I looked like a rat after it'd gotten spit out of the sewer, and she looked like a super model in the middle of a runway. I wasn't winning any glamour votes.

Day four and I still had no idea. No one gave me condescending looks anymore—now I got pity or indifference. When I pointed this out to Charles, hinting that this whole experiment into magic land was probably a mistake, he'd said, "Don't give up yet, Sasha. We'll get it. I've been thinking about when you use your magic, and I think that maybe I just need to threaten your life. That's bound to wake your magic up. I'll just, like, ruff you up a whole bunch. Or, I know—I'll get Jonas in here. If there's anyone who wants to choke the life out of you, it's Jonas. I betcha he'll spark your magic survival reflex."

He meant well.

Master Bert clapped with a beaming smile as he sashayed

into the room. "Okay, everyone, I have a special treat for you today. Maw, I have been reminded by the Boss himself that it is often easier to connect with the elements when we are out amongst them. He *personally* sought me out to tell me this!"

"Jesus, he sounds like a groupie."

Charles smirked and rolled his eyes.

"So let's go, let's go. Follow me!" Master Bert gestured everyone out through the doors.

As everyone shuffled outside—the girls all throwing red faced glances Charles's way, as usual—Charles said, "You've hit red, I don't understand the problem..."

I didn't, either.

I stepped through the backdoor of the mansion and onto a stone path. We followed the rest of the students through swaying trees, huddling in the darkness, the inky black licking my senses.

I closed my eyes as we walked, feeling that pulsing in my chest—the one I had tried to find inside, but hadn't been able to. Now, with the night looming around me, pressing on all sides, it felt like something was released. Something inside me relaxed, the block dissolving away.

Suddenly, I felt the magic crouching in Charles where he touched my back to direct me. The darkness whispered in the form of leaves rustling, of night birds calling, of the tickle of the wind as it stirred my hair. I connected with my childhood; peering through the darkness, seeking out the imaginary people. Feeling the whisper in my body, the tickle of my senses.

It had always been magic. I just hadn't known. And I attributed it to the night. I'd probably learned to control it, as Charles said, when on my own, feeling my way through the darkness.

Joy filled my body, sensing Master Bert now, a glowing orb burning within him. Onto the other students, many with tiny sparks, nothing more than colored winks, and only two with a small flame.

I stopped, eyes closed, feeling the ground beneath me. Shoes quickly shed, I stepped off the path, dirt at my feet, clutching Charles's hand and dragging him with me. His inner orb felt my petting and started to dance, spinning and twirling.

The air brushed my face, wanting to be let in. The dirt at my feet wanted to climb up my body. The heat grew, the joy making me laugh. I raised my hands, my smile twisting, electricity filling the air, humidity squeezing out water. Charles stood mute behind me, his orange orb starting to flicker brighter, a deeper color, merging with my power and intensifying.

"Isn't it wonderful?"

Was that my voice? It sounded deep and sultry, sensuous. I laughed, carefree and light, my fingers crackling with power, spikes of pain pricking my skin.

"No, Sasha!"

My body whipped around, brought into an iron chest and surrounded by bands of steel arms. The joy cut off by a control more fastidious. Somehow, my magic was smoothed out and balanced, dissolving the danger.

In opposition, my heart jumped, beating wildly in my chest. Heat filled me, but not from magic. I leaned my head against Stefan's hard chest and sighed.

"What are you playing at?" His words bounced off my head.

"I don't know, it felt wonderful. I was so happy for a minute."

"You were trying to draw too much. You have to learn to control each element before you bring them together. Most importantly, you have to learn to cut off the draw."

His heart pushed against my cheek pleasantly. "*That's* what

I did?" I backed off his chest so I could meet his intense black eyes. His handsome face took my breath away, his strength and power had me floating, his presence and charisma making me melt. It wasn't fair, this thing he did to me. It wasn't fair that his choice as mate was an equally beautiful jerk named Darla who didn't deserve him.

"How'd you know I needed to come outside?" I whispered.

His head leaned down fractionally, getting closer. "You feel things. You respond. React. You're not a planner or a plodder. I figured if you were exposed to it, your body would remember how to do it. But you have to control it. It was dangerous what you just did. You know what happens when you draw too much."

"I don't..." I shook my head. "I don't know how to control it."

"That's why you're in school," he whispered, his pupils dilating. His eyes roamed my face, touching my eyes, my nose, glancing across my cheek, then to my mouth. He sucked in a deep breath, his eyelids drooping. His fingers tightened on my arms, drawing my body closer.

My hands landed on his lateral muscles, bumpy and delicious. I breathed in his smell, musk and masculine. Safety and protection.

"Boss, Bert is nearly here. This the way you want him to see you? *Damn it*, she smells good when she's turned on!"

Stefan jerked me away from him, his eyes blinking quickly as they refocused. He let me go and stepped back.

I could have kicked Charles!

Master Bert hustled up, his eyes catching me and relaxing. A second later, they hit Charles with a scowl, then hit Stefan. "Oh my gosh! Boss! What are—*hello*! Did you detain them? Maw, I feared something had happened to them, the tricky little monkeys."

"Something did." Stefan gently pushed me toward Charles. Before he took his hand away, I could have sworn his thumb brushed my collarbone. "Sasha tried to draw too much. Charles let her do it, staring at her like a googly-eyed teenager. She needs to be watched. She's above the other students in power level—dangerously so."

"Well, hmm." Master Bert put his hand to his chest in thought. "I confess, I didn't know if she could even *reach* her power. What an excellent suggestion, then, coming out here. Maw, yes. Hmm. Should I separate them? Move them up a level?"

Stefan blew out a breath. "We'll have to divide her time. Put her in more classes; speed up her education. Learn elements from you, push her to James for weapons, then to Darla for incantations."

"Not Darla," I blurted.

Stefan speared me with his Boss stare. My back and lower cheeks tingled, a warning that danger headed my way. I shut the hell up before he did something awful.

To Master Bert he said, "This starts tomorrow. Get her working. We don't have a lot of time—she's in danger every time she uses her magic without control." His bearing still filled with command, expecting to be obeyed at any cost, his next words were for me. "And no more reckless car rides. You're putting yourself in needless danger. They stop immediately."

My argument died on my lips as his powerful gaze shocked into my system. Didn't mean I agreed, though. *Easier to ask forgiveness than permission...*

"Maw, yes!" Master Bert nodded at Charles and I, still thinking about my education. "Absolutely, Boss! Your pet is safe with me."

As the words sank in, the world slowed down. My gaze swiveled to Master Bert, incredulous.

"Yes, well." Stefan turned, a flash of irritation smearing his face before he stalked off.

"Pet?" I asked Charles in a disbelieving whisper as Master Bert led the way. "Is that what he said?"

My mind flashed back to Jonas on the first night we met them. When he and Charles had called me *little pet*. They'd thought Jared and I would break down and do as they said in mindless agreement. We were only as good as our willingness to drop our pants. Dimwitted humans. Lesser species.

Anger filled me. Shaking my head and blinking, I realized that I was being led by an oblivious Charles. His thoughts weren't bent on how wrong that term was, how immoral. Quite the opposite. It was a given.

What the hell was wrong with these people?

I sucked that thought in. I tucked it away. I didn't know how to handle it yet, the pain of it—so I would stuff it in a new secret box. I'd thought that if I learned this stuff, earned my reputation, I'd fit in. Nowhere in that equation was stooping to being a *pet* human.

My chin rose as my heart fell, refusing to let that term diminish my accomplishment of sucking in elements. I'd show them I wasn't just a stupid human. I'd learn this stuff and rock their world.

Somehow.

CHAPTER TWO

CHARLES WAS IN STITCHES FOR THE REST OF THE CLASS. IT seemed that pulling in elements once was enough for Sasha to thoroughly figure out how to do it repeatedly. Other students, even the best, would need a few seconds of concentration before they had some magic flowing. Not Sasha. Not anymore. She couldn't pay attention for crap, she couldn't remember even a sentence of knowledge if she heard it, but let her work with her hands once, and she got it. Not only that, but she pulled in way too much, freaked out, and then puffed a red fog that had the ability to singe off eyebrows.

Bert had gotten less and less chipper as the class wore on. He also had less and less hair on the top of his head. It seemed Sasha could pull fire the best. Yee haw. Plus, every time she did something before Salline, the top overachiever in class, she nodded to herself. She was pitting herself against the best and keeping tabs, willing herself to be better.

Thank God, too, cause Charles was really starting to get worried. He'd heard she could turn a letter opener red when she first came here. That was a decent flow of magic. Not only that, but she had the Boss's eye. It took a special ability to have him looking—hinting at much higher than red. But up until now, she was like every other human that someone brought around to show off: fairly useless.

But what the hell was up with that strange shadow she had going on? It was like a wispy essence of the Boss hanging around her. Every time she bent over, or looked up at him in jubilation, or did something feminine, Charles would get wood. Natural enough. Except, when he thought about trying a move, he'd get a strange scent wafting by, that kinda smelled like the Boss in the height of rage. If that didn't deflate the ol' sails, Charles didn't know what would.

Great gods, Charles needed to get laid. It'd been twelve days! The crazy human had him always on his toes—he was afraid to leave her alone in case she did something stupid. Like go give the Boss the finger.

"Alright, let's go for a ride." Sasha stalked off toward the house in determination.

"Whoa, wait a minute." Charles ran to catch up, unable to help a smirk at the small curl of smoke rising from Bert's scalp. The man should've just backed away like everyone else. "The Boss said no to that."

"True. And if you aren't a snitch, we won't get caught going against his wishes."

"Sasha, no. No way." Charles grabbed her arm to keep her from marching through the gate toward the parking lot. A pure shot of lightning blasted his palm.

"Ow!" He shook his hand. "Why the hell are you sparking? What are you, a mutant?"

"No. Just a pet. Or maybe that's the same thing," she muttered softly.

He got the feeling he wasn't supposed to hear that. Her chest bowed in. He'd seen people do that in the field, closing down, trying to protect their vitals. The words, quiet and deep, hinted at a profound hurt. Something more than just taking offense to that idiot Bert. Something more than indignation, or even outrage. This was something older; old haunts that stayed with her.

Charles had noticed her look of crushed bewilderment earlier. He'd seen the dark cloud settle more firmly around her shoulders. It was heavier and darker than the previous dark cloud of failure and uncertainty. It was adding weight and pressure, which might crush her chances of becoming whatever the Boss thought she could be.

The strange thing was, Sasha seemed like such a tough, street-smart girl. She would run head-first into danger with a smile on her face, but call her a pet and she broke down. There was a sensitivity there, an uncertainty of being different and cast aside, that flowed beneath the fun-loving, brash exterior. She might play at being indestructible, but she was a person underneath it all, with the same soft spots and triggers. Charles could sympathize; he was extremely young for Watch Commander, and got poked at and ridiculed constantly. He'd spent a whole year beating the crap out of people to mask his insecurity. Sasha would beat this, too, she just had to beat a few heads first.

Maybe Charles should show her how. Later, though. For right now, he would use a little charm. He'd been studying up, watching the human romance movies. A little research and *voila*, spread legs and a happy ending. Fail proof.

"Hey," he said, careful not to touch her in case she blasted him with one of those hair eating fogs. "Did I ever tell you how beautiful you are?"

"No. You must've missed that step in your pick-up routine."

Her voice was flat. Serious, or sarcastic... It was hard to tell with her when she was in a bad mood. Probably serious— she didn't tend to joke when she was sad.

Movie rule number one: when in doubt, apologize.

"I'm sorry, that was my fault. I can be really oblivious at times. But you really are, you know. You have beautiful eyes..."

She hesitated as she reached for the door handle. Slowly, not able to help herself, she turned to him, insecurity riding her movements. Fidgety. "Yeah right. I'm ugly compared to the girls in that mansion."

Her long eyelashes fluttered and her heart-shaped lips dropped into a sensuous pout. Oh man, it would be worth it fighting that weird essence of the Boss. Charles wanted to conquer this mountain so bad, it hurt.

However, movie rule number two: he had to take it easy. Easy and sensitive—human chicks dug that.

He suppressed his grin and leaned against the car. "They have nothing underneath it. All they are is hip and breast. You are the whole package. You make me want to be a better person."

Her brows dipped in confusion as her body unconsciously swayed toward him. He straightened up a little, draping his body around her, but not touching her yet. He had her on the hook, but he hadn't reeled her in. She was skittish. He had to take his time.

"I am?" Her pout got more pronounced, uncertainty tugging at the corners of her lips.

Classic chick response. "Yes, you are. You're really sexy. I'm scared of walking away and never feeling, in my whole life, the way I feel with you right now. You get me in all the right ways. No one else affects me like you do."

Her lamb eyes blinked up at him, hopeful. Trusting. Wanting to be something special to a man, and begging him to be that guy. To give her that fantasy of happily ever after.

He bent down toward her, his face close to hers, his hands settling low on her hips. "We fit together, you and me. I like you just the way you are. We'll make magic together."

She stepped closer, unable to help herself, her eyes on his lips. Her hands, kept low, reached for him, needy. Wanting to be loved.

A surge of electricity lit up his world. His teeth welded shut and his eyes vibrated in his skull. He rolled back against the metal of the car and shimmied down the hood. Electricity frazzled his nerves and zinged out through his limbs.

"Why would you do that to me?" he yelled, spasming on the ground. "And what the hell did you just do?"

"A whistle is good, but sometimes I like the power of a Taser."

"Uuuuhhhhhh-uh." His body pulsed in a horrible way. "That's a helluva way to treat someone who's complimenting you!"

"Charles, *really?* We'd make magic together? You like me just the way I am? Why didn't you just say, 'You complete me'? And no way do I rank over the super models with crazy kick moves that walk in that house. Give me a break."

"I was trying to make you feel better!"

"By coming on to me? And, I feel fine. What are you talking about?"

The way he noticed her standing, though, with her chin raised and her face wary, it was pretty clear she did not feel fine. Charles had a feeling she was really self-conscious about something. But she was still fingering that damned Taser like her own personal bodyguard. Two words flashed through Charles head: *steer clear.*

"My mistake. Operation: Let's Get Charles Killed When the Boss Finds Out Sasha Has Defied a Direct Order is underway. Let's get this baby up to one-twenty-nine this time."

"No problem."

His balls hurt. Stupid human movies. Now he'd have to

give it some time before trying to have sex with her again. Otherwise, she may do irreparable damage.

The next day saw Bert completely hairless and extremely irritated. The man just would not back off when Sasha gritted her teeth and swore. It was his own damn fault.

The bad news was Sasha was now being ridiculed by the other students. Blasting red when no one else could surpass measly purple, hanging out with a hunk Watch Captain, and working magic in a way no one had ever heard, inspired jealousy. Jealousy inspired snide comments and the term *pet* to be thrown around constantly. The better Sasha got, the worse the comments became.

By the time the class was over, Sasha's body was rigid and her only response to her mood was *fine.*

"You don't seem fine," Charles remarked as they broke for mid-meal. With the new schedule, they got a short break before weapons.

Sasha's shrug was tense and robotic. "I don't know what to tell you. I'm fine."

"Those kids are just jealous. They're being dicks on purpose."

This shrug looked more like a weird dance. "I know. It's fine. Seriously Charles, don't worry about it—I'm fine."

"Sasha—"

"Stop staring at my boobs."

Charles yanked his gaze upwards. "Don't tell me what to do."

Her smirk vanished as the familiar forlorn expression resettled on her face. The knot in her forehead winked back into existence. Charles had realized it was her thinking cap. "I just have to get really good at this." She sighed. "Stefan is gold, and that's great. Do you want to eat outside? I don't feel like being overheard when I'm trying to remember stuff."

Charles loaded a plate with meat from the house buffet and followed her out. "The Boss is deep, burnished gold. It's the highest level before you rocket into white."

She nodded and sat, putting her plate off to the side and pulling out her notes. Charles' eyes monitored her lips as she chewed on the end of her pencil. He really wanted those lips wrapped around the head of his—

"Ow!" He rubbed his nose where she'd just snapped him with her pencil.

"Get laid, already. Focus for two seconds. So pale gold is..." Her clear hazel eyes stared at him.

"Not as strong as the Boss."

She nodded again. "The order is purple, as the lowest, blue, green, red, orange, gold, white, black."

"Explain to me why this is so hard for you to remember?"

Sasha threw him a scowl. "I've never heard any of this stuff before. You've heard it since you were a kid. Give me a break. Okay, I should be extra awesome, since I'm supposed to be black, but instead, when I do things, they seem to have the opposite effect. Like I'm doing it wrong. Or something. I can't understand Bert half the time when he tells me things."

"Wait...you're supposed to be black? Who said?"

Sasha waved it away. "I shoot black stuff in dire situations. Stefan thinks this is good news."

Huh. Yeah, that would explain a great many things with the Boss. But he'd never even *heard* of a black power level...

Back on track, he said, "Maybe you're not doing it wrong, but it's just because you pack such a wallop?"

"I use red all the time. That should be middle tier. How is that a wallop?"

"I don't know. Maybe use your normal power level and it gets easier?"

She shook her head in frustration. "That's what I mean. It doesn't seem to work like that for me. You guys struggle to pull magic when it gets closer to your power level. For me, when I get higher up there, all of a sudden it is like trying to hold back a flood. Like I am wrestling with a bear, or something. It's not the same. Why am I not the same, Charles? Why am I always different?"

Charles had one terrified moment of panic when he thought she would cry. Her eyes glistened and her body bowed in on itself, fragile and vulnerable. Dealing with a lifetime of insecurities and loneliness. He'd asked some questions during her high after those car rides—she couldn't remember actually losing her parents, but she constantly felt their absence; the hole where unconditional love was supposed to reside. Her foster family hadn't fully taken her in; they'd merely been a place to live. Her boyfriend, as her chosen family, hadn't ever really understood her. She'd always been the square peg trying to smash itself into the round hole.

Kind of like her set up right now.

Charles couldn't help his heart going out to her, but it didn't change his terror at what to do if she freaking cried! Should he pat her back, or give her a hug? Last time he tried to console a female, she got pissed off that he thought she was weak and kicked him in the face. Human women weren't as violent, though. Right? The movies always had the guys being supportive—but he'd tried going the romance movie route and that had ended horribly.

I really hope she doesn't punch me in the balls.

As the water wobbling in her eyes threatened to overflow, he scanned his plate for a place to put down his ribs. He had to do something.

Thankfully, though, a second later she shook out her shoulders and scrunched up her face, thinking again. Charles let out a sigh. She held it together this time, but the woman was a hair's breath away from losing it. He kind of hoped he wasn't around when she did. She was unpredictable.

"I can do this," she muttered.

"Okay, excellent. Let's practice the fire element one more time before we head to James for weapons. You're best at that element."

"Argh!" She threw her pencil at a tree. "Don't you listen? I always pull too much magic."

Charles knew this, but he loved watching the flame flicker in her fingers. It was neat. Besides, she always reigned herself in eventually. "Just go slow. And do not make me bald! I don't need pity sex. Well...yes I do; but I don't need pity to get sex, is what I meant. Except..."

Her eyes narrowed. "No, Charles, that wouldn't work with me, either."

"What the hell did I do to the Boss that he had to pair me with the biggest prude in the world?" He flashed her a grin. "For now."

Sasha shook her head and closed her eyes. She dropped her hands to her knees, palms up. For a second, nothing happened, and then a faint blue flame flickered over her fingers. The flame turned green slowly, working toward more power. To red, her default. Lately, she'd stopped there, too nervous to draw more.

His eyes scanned the meat in front of him. And then swept the ground for the bottle of spicy BBQ sauce. The cooks were getting the hang of BBQ, but they still shied toward bland. He had to up the ante with sauce that would curl his hair.

"Where am I?" Her voice barely rose above a whisper.

Oh yeah.

Orange flame grew along her palm, rising six inches into the sky. He felt his own power stir. She had this awesome ability to coax another person to draw more magic. At least, she could with him. It was excellent and really helpful.

"Orange. Good job."

Her breath came in fast pants. "It's trying... to...force me..."

Charles reached forward to shake her shoulders, but he still had the ribs. *Dang it!* Orange started to morph toward gold. Her eyebrows dipped low over her eyes. If he wasn't careful, soon he'd get a hairless fog!

Thinking fast, he leaned forward and slapped her across the face. Her eyes snapped open and the glow winked out. BBQ sauce smeared her cheek.

"It helped, didn't it?" Charles said with a haughty air before she had time to berate him. "And it worked way faster. I think we have a winner. No need for thanks."

Sasha leaned forward very slowly, anger burning in her eyes. She put her little hand in his palm, the heat making his dick stand on end. Suddenly his body *zinged* with a shock so strong his teeth clamped shut and his eyes bulged. The only sound he could make was, "Ahhhhhhhhheeeeeee."

She took back her hand as her smile turned smug. "Well, it helped, didn't it?"

Rubbing one palm against the other, his ribs laying on the ground, he said, "How could that have possibly helped me? And how did you do that? And look at my ribs! They have dirt and grass stuck to them."

"I wasn't trying to help you. I was helping me. And it worked—I no longer feel extremely pissed off that you slapped me, you donkey. Although, I did waste a bunch of money on a Taser I no longer need."

"You reached gold this time," he said with approval.

"Stefan's gold?"

Was it just him, or were her eyes twinkling with something like a challenge? Her goal seemed aimed toward topping the Boss. Huh.

Too bad she hadn't. "It was a lighter gold. But if you kept going..."

Her sigh deflated her chest. "I don't know—it gets too... slippery or something. Too hard to control. It's like the elements all try to rush me. Like I'm walking on a knife blade while juggling fire. I don't want to get magic shock..."

Good point. Charles hadn't thought about that. Usually a person only got magic shock when teamed with two or more other people for a large spell or incantation. The group had to be careful to centralize the flow so no one individual got a larger dump of magic. Since the Boss took power of the clan, though, he usually joined those circles and balanced everything out. It was one of his special, natural abilities that proved advantageous to the clan—they could form larger circles and construct more advanced spells with him involved. Rarely anyone got magic shock anymore.

Only, Sasha could apparently get it on her own. Charles couldn't even imagine how frustrating that must be. To constantly have to watch your own back from pulling in too much. Also, that it was possible.

Once again, Charles couldn't help but wonder what the Boss had found.

Nor could he salvage his dinner.

He chose to worry about his stomach for the moment. Let the Boss handle the prickly human.

Grumbling, he went back inside to refill his plate.

*****

"That is your dagger. Your dagger is your best friend. You take your dagger everywhere with you. You sleep with your dagger. You know your dagger like the back of your hand. When you are in trouble, your dagger will save you. Do I make myself understood?"

I raised my hand slowly from the back of the large, bare room in the basement of the mansion. Weapons of all kinds glittered on the walls in the dim light, screaming violence. A cluster of tall students stood in front of me holding their daggers, gripping them with assurance. With a speech like that, not having a dagger or knife would present a serious problem.

I had a serious problem.

"Yes, the human in the back." James was a robust man with salt and pepper hair and a grim face. He stood on a platform, his thick arms wound around his back in faux patience as he looked over his troops.

"Umm," I froze as the students, older than the elements class but still not quite my age, gawked. More than one snickered. "I haven't been issued a dagger."

"Oops." Charles scratched his nose.

James stared for a moment, his deep brown eyes flat. Finally, he tweaked his head toward the wall o' death. "Get one."

"Yup. Okay." I hurried over and reached out for a smallish blade—until I noticed a skull on its hilt.

"Yuck," my hand flinched back. I scanned the area surrounding it, seeing every type of sharp object in existence. Great, curved blades gleamed against the gray wall, heavy and intense. Not for me. I moved down, noticing a polished wood stick with a chain leading from the tip. At the end of the chain was a ball with spikes. I grimaced again. Finally my eyes settled on a dagger about the length of my forearm with a straight hilt and no frills.

As I grabbed the hilt and pulled it from the wall, the expertly polished handle slipped. The blade went skittering across the floor, straight at the center of the class.

"Crap!" I screeched.

"Great gods, jump!" James shouted.

Barely missing the ankles of a beautiful, redheaded girl, the blade did a pirouette, sparkling for a second in the dim lighting before it stilled.

"Sorry!" I held up my hand to ward off the death glare from James. "It's my first day."

"Have you ever even *held* a dagger, human?" James asked with a mystified voice.

"Or should we call you *pet?*" the redhead asked with a sneer.

The term punched me. I'd just chosen my new mortal enemy overachiever. I would be better than her at this stuff if it killed me.

I frowned, but didn't say anything. I did almost chop the girl's foot off. I kind of deserved that comment. Still, though...she better look out. I was gunning for her.

"Once," I answered James quietly. "I used it in the battle not that long ago. Or fight? I don't know what you guys call it? Before that, I used a letter opener because I didn't have anything else on me at the time. Besides a whistle. The whistle actually came in handy. Surprisingly..."

Charles' forehead hit his palm.

"You were in the battle?" A sandy haired boy smirked at me, nudging a black haired boy standing next to him. "Doing what? Hiding under your master's bed?"

He also just made the list.

James clapped, quieting the snickers, but not dislodging the sneers. "Fine, pick up your weapon. You are way behind, but apparently one of the undisclosed higher-powers thought you needed to start this class right now, rather than waiting the few weeks until Mira starts the next one, so I guess we'll have to do."

Oh yeah, great. Thanks, James, for pointing that out. My classmates don't hate me enough as it is...

Suppressing a grumble, I scooped up my dagger.

"Showboat," Charles whispered under his breath, eyeing a lovely blonde with giant boobs.

"Like I meant to sever toes," I snapped, trying to pay attention as James spoke about elements and metals and God only knew what.

"Okay, practice." James clapped again. That must've been his thing. Clapping.

It was better than that weird *maw* sound Master Bert made.

"What am I practicing?" I asked Charles out of the side of my mouth.

Charles backed away quickly as James stepped up beside me. "Problem?"

My face heated. "Oh, no. Not at all, no. I was just..."

James' eyebrows nudged his hair line.

"Turning the blade a color?" I finished hopefully.

"You are infusing your blade with power. If you are able to do it, your blade will turn a color, yes. Probably a lovely shade of purple, if you're lucky."

Riiight.

I glanced around. Everyone else had their blades basically glowing, with only a few still working on it. None of them showed any real strength at it, though. Not like Charles or Stefan—

My groin swelled and my sexy systems started to ache. Since I'd seen him earlier, the craving had come back in force. His smell, his hard chest, his—

"What is that...smell..." James glanced around, trying to identify it. "Warm cookies fresh out of the oven. Delicious."

Two other men looked our way, sniffing.

"Okay, glowing sword, coming right up." I closed my eyes, belatedly remembering that this was a different exercise than the fire element one I'd just practiced, and tried to shift gears. Too late. A sudden onslaught of power flooded me. It sneaked in from everywhere, boosting my power-level and clawing at my middle. Joy, heat, bliss, lava—

Too much. I needed brakes!

A large palm met my cheek with surprising force. My head whipped around, power sizzling through my body and out through my limbs, finding release.

Everyone gasped.

I opened my eyes to a flaming sword. Bright red light streaked out of the tip and zipped into the ceiling above, tearing a shallow hole before soaking into the walls.

"Thank God it was pointing up," I whispered with shock.

"Who sent you here, human?" James asked in a suspicious voice. His eyes swiveled to Charles, for the first time realizing I had a guard, not a fellow classmate. If there was one thing Charles did not need help with, it was operating a sword.

Either of his swords, actually. Just ask him.

"That's classified?" I hedged.

"As you can see," Charles spoke up, vaguely gesturing toward the hole in the ceiling, "she is a danger to herself and others. We identified her and had to bring her here until trained."

"Oh, great, a *dangerous* pet. Who was the idiot who found her?"

I scowled at that sandy haired twerp who couldn't keep his yapper shut.

"Me." Charles straightened dramatically, the tattoos peeking out from under his shirt sleeves. Easily the tallest in the class, and certainly the most filled out, Charles was a stack of destructive muscle with a dangerous edge. His smoky gray eyes flashed with danger, his striking face drawing eyes. "I was doing my job as the Watch Captain."

A few girls gasped and more than one guy shifted insecurely. When Charles wanted to put on a show, he stopped traffic.

"Class, class." *Clap, clap, clap.* "Let's get back to it. Sasha, you are excused. You are too dangerous for this class. Tell your master you will need to wait for Mira."

My intestines iced over. Not only did he assume I had a master, like a slave, but he was sending me away without instruction. If I wasn't taught, I'd surely fail. If this guy turned me away, the next instructor probably would, too. "But, I need to learn this..."

"That isn't my problem," James retorted, unconcerned. "I can't have you killing a student because you can't listen. Out you get."

"James, really *look* at her for a second," Charles murmured. "Take a big whiff."

Before I could ask what that was about, James indignantly surveyed me. He leaned forward and inhaled. "What..." His eyebrows rumbled, prompting closer examination. "Why does it smell faintly of..."

Suddenly his face drained of color and he took a step back. "Mmm, yes, higher-level, I see." He turned to Charles and offered a light bow. "She should probably stay. It isn't distinctly clear that this is his property, hence my not noticing it at first, but...yes. I apologize—I was not aware the Boss took a pet."

Ice turned slowly into fire. I needed instruction, yes, but I had my pride. Which this man, and Stefan, were stepping on.

I'd had enough. Of all of this. My whole life I'd tried to

keep half of myself from people. Tried to hide and save face. Feared to completely be myself.

Well, screw that. I was sick of it. I didn't lose my old life to end up in the same rut!

Fire surged, feeding off the last week of fear and uncertainty.

One big tear wobbled down my face. The redheaded girl laughed and said, "Uh oh, poor baby's going to run to her *master*."

Yes, I sure was. I was going to pull this weed out by the root. Then I might come back and punch her squarely in the jaw.

I pushed the pain of defeat down; let it harden my resolve. *Let's dance, Stefan!*

"Where are you going?" Charles asked as the knuckles around my dagger turned white.

"To light some fireworks."

If I didn't stand up for myself, then what did I have left? Nothing. I'd be useless *and* broken.

My sword flashed a bright gold, my wobbly emotions not applying the brakes to the flow of magic.

"Sasha," Charles said, warning in his voice. "Crying is probably better."

My dagger started to smoke. Charles worried that too much magic was trying to force its way in. It wasn't. For some reason I couldn't explain, I had complete control. But then, I was heading into danger. That had always been the recipe, had it not? I rose to the occasion when there was surviving to do.

Didn't matter why, though; I had an agenda.

Past reason, I turned to Charles, my blade deepening in color. I opened myself up a crack more. Smoke billowed now, the blade grinning madly as its color pushed into a deep gold.

"If I were you, I would get lost. This is probably one of the stupidest things I've ever done."

"Then why are you grinning? You know I can't, Sasha. Don't do this," Charles pleaded.

Before I exited the large classroom, I leveled with him. "Do you think I'm his pet, Charles? Do you think I'm here because he has a sexual interest in me?"

The large man hesitated, glancing back at the spectators.

"All rightie, then. Good chat." I about-faced.

My blade turned a molten, burnished gold. The color of Stefan's power. Let everyone see we were equal.

In power level, anyway.

Consulting my inner guide, also known as that nagging part of me that always strived to reach Stefan and was always aware of his presence, I turned my body toward the center of the house. The sun peeked out from behind the horizon, splattering my face and lifting my spirits. I loved the darkness, but I also craved the light. The night called to my magic, the day to my spirit.

Focusing on that part deep inside me that connected with Stefan, I brought it out and held it up, analyzing it. Analyzing him.

He worried. Something troubled him. Fear ate at the corners of his brain, distracting him.

I opened a large white door, the wood swinging on silent hinges. He had just stood up from his seat around a large table, eyes expectant, knowing I'd be walking in. Everyone else at the table followed his gaze. He held his sword in his left hand.

"Sasha, you need to calm down. Whatever's the matter, we can discuss it." He sounded so calm. A human lunatic with a knife wanted to poke holes in his stupid body, and he addressed me as if I asked about a petition.

"Is her dagger white?" someone whispered. Another gasped.

"Is she Trek's creation? Is he controlling her?" a lady trilled.

He had been in the middle of a meeting. I didn't care.

I had the knife, the power, the anger, the angst...I just needed a way to begin the duel. Somehow *olé* didn't seem appropriate. Maybe I should slap him with a white glove...

"Can we speak of this in private?" Stefan tried again.

"Why, so you can pat me on the head, put me in chains, and tell everyone what a great pet I am?"

"They've been calling her pet all week, Boss," Charles mumbled from the door. "Should I remove her?"

"Try it, Charles. Try to remove his majesty's pet. See what happens." Pain threatened to consume me, wobbling my lower lip. A single tear worked out of my eye. *Not the time for vulnerability!*

"This clan knows I do not take pets. I do not adhere to that practice." Stefan stood tall, that danged connection calling me. Begging me to step forward and merge my body with his. To find the peace I sought within his arms.

I took a step back, my heart dropping an inch. My chest filled with lead, covering over that connection. Hiding it.

Stefan took a step, a strange apprehension peeking through his controlled mask. "What did you just do?"

"I've thought about your earlier offer for room and board. Thank you, but I decline. I think I'll take my chances on my own."

The door slammed behind me. Charles stood in front of it with a grim face and sorrowful eyes. He shook his head. "I can't let you run away, Sasha. You remember what happened the last time."

"We can't let the enemy get hold of you." Stefan's voice grated. "They're searching. You've nearly died by their hand twice. It's me you have the problem with. Come with me now, we'll speak about this."

"So I'm a prisoner, is that it?"

"This is your home, now."

"Living with a bunch of people who think I am a possession does not make this my home. Tell me, Stefan, how would you feel if your *home* consisted of a bunch of people who thought you were no better than someone's dog? A dangerous dog, at that. A prized trophy, guarded constantly. They probably think I'm a sex slave, too. Can't learn magic, human, no skills—I don't belong here. I hear it all the time. I didn't belong in my old life, either. Not with my old family, not with my old boyfriend—what does that make me, Stefan?" Pain welled up from down deep. "Unwanted. How could this possibly be a home?" *Will I ever have one? Will I ever fit?*

Stefan stared at me grimly.

The lethal poise of the Boss's body shook my confidence. Flouting his dominance in front of his subjects was definitely the stupidest thing I'd ever done, and I'd done some pretty eyebrow raising stuff. He wasn't a guy I would fight and live long enough to gossip about. I needed to go, and I did not plan to let Charles the Double Crosser bar my way. Not ever again.

"Move, Charles, or I will move you."

Pity overcame his expression. "This is best for you, Sasha. You have to see that."

"This is the second time I ask. There will not be a third. Please move."

"Sasha." Stefan took another step toward me. His face held a command, stern and disapproving.

"Just beguile her," someone said with exasperation. "Make her listen. Your plaything is out of control, Boss, excuse me for saying. She—"

Way wrong term.

I turned with a now-black blade, my other hand outstretched, pointing at a man with a round face and double chin. Black smoke surrounded him, binding him to his chair. Magic taxed my body, prickling my skin with heat. I was close to the cusp. I pushed my palm through the air. His chair flew backward, knocking a lamp and globe out of the way before hitting, then putting a hole through, the wall behind him.

"If you do not stop this right now, I will be forced to stop you." Stefan had his sword up. The tattoos on his arms glowed that burnished gold.

It felt as if something scrabbled through my chest. He searched for the link. He could use it to smother my magic. And he would. He could control all of this. He knew how to work the elements just so, how to build—whatever Master Bert had said—and hone...that other thing. He operated with calm and level-headed knowledge.

I operated by the seat of my pants. I'd been lucky so far. My butt tingle told me it was about to end.

A wildness crept into me, something primal and fierce. I moved like a rabid animal from a net. Pointing my sword at the door, I blasted a hole through the handle, turning my blade back to white; I didn't have much stamina—magic required energy to use and sustain. Like a runner, you had to work at endurance. I hadn't been at this for long.

Charles stood his ground with the grim faced courage he was known for throughout the clan. I darted at him, slapping my hand against his arm, and electrifying it as I did so. He flew sideways as if from an explosion.

A quick glance told me Stefan had started running, seeing that my escape attempt would work.

"Sasha, please, *don't*!" he shouted.

Too late.

Already weakening, I ran like the devil was chasing me, lighting through the hallways, rooms, and corridors, letting my inner compass guide me. It had never led me astray, even before all this magic mumbo-jumbo, and I trusted it now.

I burst out of the doors into the bright sunlight, my vision a cloud of white while my pupils tried to contract. I stumbled, hitting a tree and falling to my knees. Up a second later, shouting sounding off behind me, I started to run, no destination in mind.

CHAPTER THREE

STEFAN EXPLODED INTO THE SUNLIGHT AND IMMEDIATELY had to shield his eyes, the rays like daggers stabbing into the back of his skull. Someone handed him sunglasses. He straightened up slowly, still squinting, working at that damn link. She shouldn't have been able to disguise it. That wasn't how it worked.

"Which direction, Boss?" Charles asked, stepping to his side. His voice held traces of worry. He'd grown attached.

Stefan shook his head, scanning the tree line. "Woods, but I have no idea where. I can't..." He shook his head again.

"What does a black blade mean?" Jameson asked. "I haven't heard of black. Is it between white and gold?"

"It's a step beyond white."

"Couldn't be." Jameson stepped to Stefan's other side. He didn't care about the human—about Sasha—but he had figured out Stefan's claim on her, the soft mark, and knew she was important in some way. For that alone, Jameson would rally. He was a solid choice as Second.

"That's a myth," Jameson stated.

"You were in that room," Stefan said simply, working at

that damn link. When her power faltered, he'd uncover it. He'd find her. He just hoped it wasn't too late.

"Theatrics?" Jameson walked forward, eyes low on a tree trunk.

"She'd just picked that blade off the wall at random," Charles said, shaking his head. "It wasn't theatrics. She's been doing weird things. Weird magic. Bert is flabbergasted. James probably is, too, though he only saw it for a second. She took that pet stuff very...badly."

Charles, the fucking master observer.

"I can track her." Jameson slowly walked to the tree line. "She didn't take it easy. Her footprints are messy."

"Do it!"

"If she has black magic, she could turn the war..." Jameson let the thought trail away.

"She's completely untrained." Stefan's eyes searched the ground behind Jameson, finding a shoe print. "She was the one who disbanded all the *Dulca* in the battle, I'm sure of it. They react to her, are drawn to her magic. They *speak* to her in a language she can understand."

Jameson straightened and looked back at him, his face clouding with uncertainty. It was Charles who responded to the silent accusation.

"She isn't working for Trek. She's barely working for herself, and she has a vested interest in staying alive. She learns incredibly fast with hands-on, but try to explain something to her and at the end of your sermon, she'll still be looking at a flower instead of you, completely oblivious. She isn't a spy. Definitely is *not* a spy."

"How can you be sure? Spies are deceptive..."

Charles laughed. "Yeah, she's deceptive, all right. You'll think she'll say or do one thing, then she does something else entirely, not even knowing why herself. No, spend any amount of time with her. That chick ain't no spy!"

Jameson shook his head, his glance passing by Stefan. He worried. Hell, so did Stefan in the beginning.

The blockage cleared suddenly, and just like that, he felt her again. Her misery, her depression, her utter hopelessness. Stefan's heart constricted. He started to run.

*****

I came awake slowly, my body sore and the grief still fresh. I'd run for a while, blasting through underbrush and dodging around trees, but my directionless plight finally sank in. Until I got on my feet, I needed Stefan's hospitality. The only other people who could possibly take me in were my foster family, and they'd already done so much of that my whole life, I couldn't ask for more.

Hopelessness washed over me again. I needed to get a job. I had to quit the crappy school job I had when I took up this gig. I had renter's insurance, so I probably had some sort of money coming my way, but I needed a steady income to live. That was probably step one. Except, there was that tiny problem of monsters tracking me down and dragging me away to a group of people even less hospitable than Stefan's clan...

Sitting up painfully, having slept for an indiscriminate amount of time on jagged rocks, I sensed a presence in the failing evening light. My head swung to the left as my midsection gave a lurch. I recognized the supportive, luring feeling of the link between us before my eyes hit his perfect face. Stefan stood some ten feet away, leaning against the tree, staring at me with his striking, dark eyes.

My body immediately leaned forward, wanting to go to him as I always had before. My mind, however, rebelled.

"You're angry." His voice was so deep and thick. It coated me in pleasure just by reaching my ears.

I mentally slapped myself and retorted, "Did the scowl give me away?"

"That was one indication, yes. Plus, I can feel you as you can feel me. I can sense you as you can sense me. Always have been able to, but now it's clearer since you've taken large quantities of my blood in a short period of time."

No problem. I imagined myself lifting a giant, rubber drain stop and smothering that blasted pit in my chest that constantly asked to be filled with him. I may learn incredibly slowly, but eventually I do learn, and since doing it in the height of my emotional crazy, I knew what to do now.

His head tilted and his eyes hardened. "That trick is not supposed to be possible. How do you do it?"

"A woman never tells."

His eyebrows lowered a fraction, his long black lashes casting shadows over his eyes as the sun disappeared behind the horizon. I'd lost a whole day atop a pile of rocks. "I wish you would leave it open. Let the connection last. It's comforting."

"So you know I'm not in enemy hands? That I'm right under your nose where you can keep tabs on me? Like a *pet.*"

"Yes. Be thankful it isn't a shock collar."

His chiseled face remained impassive, as did his eyes. I couldn't tell if he was joking.

Lifting my chin like it didn't matter, I climbed to my feet and dusted myself off. "Well, you'll be happy to know I have decided to stay on for a while until I can sort myself out. I will put up with your crap—to some extent. I will take the classes, and I will even bear the a-holes who call me your pet."

"I am delighted to hear it."

Again with the impassive delivery. It was almost as if he mocked me somehow. Or shared a joke that I didn't find funny. This was unfamiliar ground with him. Usually, he was stodgy and leader-like—super commanding and dominating. And while he was still dominating (that trait seemed built-in) he seemed more relaxed. Relaxed enough to joke?

Did he joke?

I surged on with my agenda. "I'll only be around for a while, though. And when I want to leave, I'm leaving. You know I can."

He studied me for a long moment. "I don't usually have this much problem with minions following orders."

His eyes twinkled, which didn't stop my eyebrows from lowering dangerously.

A strange flash of guilt covered his face before the wisps of a smile died. He sighed. "Look, let me be honest with you. You have an extremely rare type of magic, a powerful magic, which makes you extremely valuable. Both to my clan, and to our larger organization as a whole. You come at exactly the right time, because we badly need someone to take on Trek, the Eastern Territory's mage. We both need you trained—you and me—because without it, you run the risk of doing too much and killing yourself. You've been in that situation twice."

I crossed my arms over my chest. He didn't need to remind me.

"There's nothing I can do about others calling you a pet," he went on. "It's a stigma with humans. We see so few of them, and those can always be so easily manipulated, they do become a pet, of sorts. They usually have low ranking power. As such, they are sniffed at. Being labeled as *my* pet, you have some clout. Now, with the type of magic you possess, and your value, you will have even more. But that stigma will be a slow thing to erode. I cannot counter that. Anything I do or say will be passed off as my affection for you. We all have a hard road. You are no different."

"I'm homeless. Charles burnt all my possessions. I'm hated. I now sound like a whining jackass—a little compassion might be nice."

The wisps of a smile were back. He apparently found my black moods humorous. "An account has been opened for you. Funds have been deposited for your employment within this clan, as a mage in training, and as recompense for Charles' accidental...sabotage. Buy new possessions."

"I can't buy new memories."

"No, but with a computer, you can re-download your photos. Or did you not back up to the cloud?"

Oh yeah. I had. I had signed up with my new computer before I even knew what I was signing up for. Then it just kept backing up there because I didn't know how to stop it.

Fate was getting awfully nosy.

Sensing a losing battle, my eyebrows lowered again. "Okay, why are you hiding me away in a secret residence?"

"We have a leak somewhere in my clan. The enemy seems to know important information they shouldn't. I don't want you accessible. They know I protect you, which means they know you have value. Now that you've demonstrated your kind of power, they'll pull the walls down to get you. You, me, and Charles know where you stay. For your own safety, that needs to remain between us, alone."

"Why are you always such a dick to me in front of others?" I fired next, trying to unsettle his perfectly calm demeanor.

A large breath escaped his mouth in a *whoosh*. He shook his head, the first sign that he didn't sit on top of the world like he pretended. Guilt flashed again, my curiosity starting to get out of control as to why. "I suddenly regret this honest discussion."

He put his hands on his hips and leaned against a tree,

looking out at the falling night. "You're...different. You affect me differently than others. As I affect you..."

His eyes swung toward me, the question in that statement ringing through the night. I stepped closer before I could help myself.

Eyes on my face, he continued, "But I'm the leader of his clan; all decisions go through me. I'm responsible for every single member's life, wellbeing, and prosperity. At first, you were nothing more than an intriguing nuisance with strange and puzzling human traits. You've come up against our human stigma first hand. I admit, it darkened my thoughts."

I scrubbed my palm against my jeans. "And now?"

His eyes bore into mine. A decision rumbled around in his head. The pause lengthened, the approaching night muffling the sounds of day, muting the light.

"I..." Something clicked into place. His face hardened. "I'm still a leader, and I have obligations. I need to take on a mate. To stabilize my role, give my clan another means to resolve problems, and continue my line through the offspring of my chosen. As I've said a few times, I don't take pets, whether my own race or yours."

"You're a one woman kind of guy? I find that hard to believe in this place..." My eyes started to sting and I had no idea why.

"I prefer the solidarity of one mate, yes. Although that's not the norm, no. You're right. Not for me until lately, and I certainly can't expect that from my future mate." His jaw clenched.

"I don't understand why you need someone with a mate title to have a few kids. Charles explained it like you guys were good with just creating kids randomly."

"Charles is young. He's flippant in his execution of our customs. My children may not carry my genetics, but through a union, they'd be born to my mantle. I'd provide for them as my own. Regardless, the clan needs a pair. A steady, stable pair. It's how it's always been. Similar to your kings and queens, arranged mating is not unusual. Many factors go into the choice. Reproduction is one, yes. As is ability to lead, politics, magical power, lineage as it concerns magical power..."

"Darla is your chosen." My heart filled with lead and squished down into my shoes. I knew that, but I needed to hear it from his mouth, once and for all.

Stefan stared at me, his face unreadable. "She is the most acceptable candidate."

That was a professional answer.

"When does this happen?"

"I should've made the decision before now. It needs to be formalized soon. The Regional needs to approve of my final choice. He's scheduled to visit in a few months' time."

I shook my head as my eyes trained on a spot of dirt next to my shoe. "How does that concern me? Why can't you just be nice? Friendly?"

"You were a distraction. A pleasant one, but not one I could allow to take my attention away from my clan. Now that you're an asset, you are under my protection. Your prosperity and overall comfort are my responsibility. I now treat you no differently than anyone else under my care. Except for this discussion. And for my checking up on you... Sometimes."

Not as professional.

"And except Darla," I muttered sulkily, wishing I'd just shut up for once.

"I treat you no differently than anyone else under my care."

I glanced up, startled. His hand was out, directing me in front of him. "Please, walk with me."

I trudged forward, my lingering sulkiness immature, but

not something I could help. Somewhere deep inside me, I knew I belonged with him. My body tried to merge with him as its other half. Being near him, next to him, touching him, sent me into an unexplainable euphoria. I'd felt it that night on the street, even having never seen his face before that moment. To now hear that that door was closed, that I couldn't even have him as a strictly sexual situation—even though that would only satisfy part of the hunger—was like a punch to the gut. It ripped at me.

"I realize that, in your situation, it seems impossible to ever make this your home." His footsteps were light even though his body's size was just shy of daunting. "But when you have more training under your belt, and can protect yourself reasonably, we can let you out of your cage."

A glance told me that he did, in fact, joke. I blinked at his smile, the effect pushing out an inner light within him that rendered me speechless.

His gaze drifted to mine, his smile losing focus.

I blurted, "I didn't think you had a sense of humor."

His gaze got more acute. "Officially, I don't."

"Do you ever get to let your hair down?"

"Can't. Too short."

"Ah. Now I see why you don't joke. Lack of material."

His lips tugged upward a little more. Then drooped again. "I don't have a lot of time that's my own. My race is one of bred hunters. I maintain my position through calculating threat and violence. If I'm challenged, I must meet that challenge and disable my opponent."

"Like a lion in charge of a pride?"

"Exactly. It doesn't leave a lot of room for laughter."

"People think a laughing man is a weak man?"

"Not weak, per se, but not alert. Not serious. They peg him as vulnerable."

"Then I better get good at what I do so I can tell some

jokes. I'll be ready with a wallop so you can laugh at my sparkling wit."

"You better get good at what you do, *and* find some sparkling wit. Uphill climb in your future."

"Go back to official. Your jokes are the pits."

He chuckled quietly.

We crossed the threshold of my hidden domain and he halted and turned to me. His eyes were intense, but puffy, and it occurred to me he'd taken vigil, watching over me as I slept. He'd been up for about twenty-four hours, and if I knew him at all, he wouldn't go to sleep now. Not with another night of duties to get through.

His large, broad shoulders squared to my body. He leaned at the waist, his face coming within inches of mine. His hand came up, fingers lightly grazing my jaw. "Please open the link. It's comforting knowing you're okay." The heat from his sweet breath ruffled my eyelashes. His smell and presence permeated my head, making me dizzy, setting my body on fire.

I tugged away that big rubber stopper, opening up to him, *feeling* him. A moan got trapped in my throat as my hand found its way to his hard pec.

He burned with arousal. That heat was tempered with regret, however. He didn't want to turn me into the pet everyone thought I was. He didn't want to use, and then discard me, knowing his choice had to lie elsewhere.

What a cute sentiment. Best left for another time, though, I needed him with a passion that took my breath away.

I reached up on tippy-toes, my lips aiming for his, my hand slipping down that mouth-watering body and cupping his huge, hard bulge. Applying pressure, I guided my other hand around him, drawing him near.

I met resistance.

"No." He shook his head, his eyes closing, inhaling my scent of arousal. "I want you to rise on your own. I want you to excel without my influence. I want you to earn the respect you deserve."

"Good call. I'm in. First, can we just knock this out? I'll be quick, I promise."

His lips quirked at the corners. "You sound like Charles."

"I might hurt you for that comment."

"Hmm." His eyes closed again, his smile growing. "If only. This is the best smell to date. Gingerbread cookies in front of a wood burning fire on Christmas Eve."

"That's a scene, not a smell."

"It's my favorite scene, the one before I lost my parents. I remember the smells perfectly." His eyes met mine, somber, but soft. "I must go. Duty."

Suddenly, I stood in the middle of a hallway, sconces throwing next to no light into my path, alone. He'd ripped his presence away so fast, I didn't even see him go. My groin felt so tight, it hurt.

"What a tease," I muttered.

"Not much of a man to leave a woman hang--"

I jumped and flung my hand out, a red jet bursting forth, flaying the wall twenty feet away. Charles rolled into the middle of the floor, on his back, hands out in surrender. "I'm just saying! I totally would've hit that—ten minutes of bump and grind, and you both feel better. Why am I the bad guy right now?"

"Were you eavesdropping the whole time?" I screeched. "That was a private moment!"

"What did you want me to do, plug my ears?"

"Ever thought of walking a-*way*?"

"I thought I'd get to witness a sex scene! No *way* am I walking away from that."

I sighed, my hands dropping to my sides and my heart still

trying to punch through my chest. "Why wouldn't he go through with it?"

"He said—duty. Boss is a man of his word. That cat sticks to his guns. He doesn't want to make a mockery of you, and judging by the fact that you nearly killed somebody by blasting him through a wall, he knows to tread lightly. That means keeping his dick in his pants, apparently. I'm glad I don't have his job."

"Like anyone would've known we bumped uglies. Except my peeping-tom protector."

"Our sense of smell is *ten* times better than humans, and the sex smell lingers. Hmm." Charles closed his eyes and stroked himself through his jeans. "I am so damn turned on right now. Anyway, everyone knows he was with you all day. Who else would it be? Plus, you have a unique scent. It changes for each person, I think. I've been cataloguing. And females can't seem to smell it."

"You are now babbling. Go have sex. I'll stay in my room."

Charles's face lit up. "Promise? Wait...sex with others, right? Or did you mean with you?" A hopeful twinkle sparked in his eyes.

"Others, you nincompoop. Get out of here."

"Okay, thanks." He stopped halfway through flight and stuck his finger out. "I can trust you, right?"

I waved him away and headed for a couple hours sleep before I had to be in class. "Go! Just do a thorough job." As I shut the door, my mind drifted back to what Stefan had said earlier, about losing his parents. I wanted to know more.

"How'd it go?" I asked as I strapped on a boot and straightened up, watching with a grin as Charles leaned with his full body against the door. I was still tired, but those couple hours of sleep were greatly needed.

"I'm *exhausted*. I found Bernise, a hot little number who can work wonders with her mouth. But then, as she got started, her friend Cheryl comes lumbering in. I'm not a huge fan of Cheryl—she's okay, don't get me wrong, but kind of a bitch. Anyway, Cheryl wants to join in. I'm hot, no two ways about it. So, now I gotta pleasure *two* girls. Being that I have a reputation to uphold, I have to work my ass off to get them to orgasm! Which meant I had to get hard multiple times in a short period of time. Eh!" He wiped his forehead of sweat.

Only young men could be this ridiculous. I grabbed a long sleeve tee to throw over my tank top. "But it worked out, I take it."

"In the end, yeah. Multiple times. But there was a weird moment—" Charles opened the door for me and waited until I walked through before continuing. "—when Jim sauntered on in. Seeing the action unfold, and the position we were in at the time, he thought he might just give me a little poke in the backside—kind of work me from both ends."

Charles stumbled, his eyes raking around. I immediately put both hands up in a double-stop gesture as I shook my head. "I have no idea why a strange orgy suddenly turned me on, okay? I'm sexually frustrated. Leave it be."

Charles grinned. "Mental note."

"Shut up."

We walked into Master Bert's training room and found a bunch of gawking kids. Their mouths hung open as they stared at us with wide eyes. Master Bert bustled up immediately. "Hello, hello! Maw, I had no idea I was working with so much power. I've been going about it all wrong. I've got someone coming in especially for you today, Sasha. If you'll just walk out the back and wait by the nearest tree, he'll be in shortly."

"Special treatment, or fear that I am insane?" I muttered to Charles.

"Insanity, probably," he replied as we found the tree. "No one has challenged the Boss like you did and lived to tell the tale."

"What does he usually do?"

"Hurt them badly, or kill them, depending on the infraction."

"*Kill* them?"

"We play for keeps. He hasn't killed anyone since his first couple of years as leader, though. Everyone got the hint."

We weren't waiting two minutes before an attractive man about my age, relatively speaking, approached with a glide. His toned body was decked out in trendy clothes, his face making the spit dry up in my mouth. Attractive little bugger.

"Sasha?" His musical, midrange voice tickled my ears.

"Y-yes," I answered, smoothing my shirt, despite the fact that it was cotton and didn't need smoothing.

"I'm Jessiah." His vibrant blue eyes shifted to Charles. "And your bodyguard?"

Charles went rigid. Apparently being called a bodyguard was a sore spot. "She's valuable. I'm doing my duty as Watch Commander and ensuring her survival."

"Ah." Jessiah smirked and lowered in front of me, matching my cross-legged style of sitting. His eyes attached to mine, an inherent sultry quality suggesting I remove my clothes for the occasion. "You are the Boss' pet, did I hear that right?"

"Way wrong thing to say, bro," Charles mumbled, shaking his head. "Especially when she's working with magic."

"Hmm. Maybe I am mistaken."

And maybe you'll get punched right in the throat! Right after I cop a feel.

"Shall we begin?" I asked sweetly.

His smile was sardonic. "Of course."

*****

Charles waited in relative boredom for Sasha to make her dagger turn a rainbow of colors. Unlike the others in the class, she didn't even have to try anymore. The elements session with Mr. Smooth Talking Jackass had her able to pull the various elements, mixing and matching as she needed, and working with what she found. Whether unconsciously, or out of fear, she only pulled enough power to reach the orange level, and that was only once. Usually she stayed in her default red. He'd asked her about it, of course, and she'd replied that Mr. Women-Love-Me made her nervous.

Charles didn't know why—that jerk wasn't packing much *and* he didn't know how to use it! When Charles tried to explain this, he got an eye roll, of all things.

Plus, the Boss would not take too favorably to his special interest taking up with Mr. I-Smooth-Out-My-Eyebrows. The guy was great at working with elements, sure, but could he do any practical magic with it? Nope. He'd tried to get into the Watch Command twice. The Boss turned him down flat both times.

Clap, clap, clap.

"Okay, let's learn some practical knowledge. Pair off." James glanced at Charles. Charles stared back. He wasn't in the mood to play babysitter to a bunch of newbies.

James backed down immediately. Yet another guy with knowledge that didn't go beyond the classroom.

Sasha's constant partner, Gabe, stared at her with nervous eyes and a line for a mouth. This was when things could get hairy. Sasha actually had great sword work, strangely enough, but with so much power zinging around her body, half the time her sword exploded. The amazing thing was that they used practice swords with no real edge—certainly not sharp. But they were metal, and could conduct energy—that was all Sasha seemed to need.

Gabe came at her at a snail's pace—the kid wouldn't go into work as a fighter, that was for sure—and slashed at her chest. She stepped out of the way like someone born for the role, and swiped at his arm plate, connecting with a scrape.

"Nice work, human. You are coming along," James said, his eyes sweeping the students.

Sasha glared at him, and then glanced beyond him to that smirking redhead she had a vendetta against. She rightly assumed she'd earned a name at this point. She was one of the best in the class with hands-on, only failing because of the flaming sword issue, which the Boss suspected had something to do with her kind of magic and not her learning ability. Half the students grudgingly accepted her, acknowledging her right to be there. The other half only smirked when she wasn't looking.

Like that redhead.

"Let's see you do it, Ginger," Sasha muttered at her enemy. Who was actually named Tessie.

The other female sneered, looking back at her sword. Charles chuckled. A little competition was good for the soul. As was beating heads, just like he'd said.

"Oh, God, sorry!"

Charles crossed his hands over his chest and watched as

Sasha laid her hands on Gabe's back. He was bent over painfully, holding his stomach. She'd probably blasted him in her anger at James-the-Clapping-Moron.

"Do what, kill my partner?" the redhead disparaged.

"I'm good, I'm good." Gabe waved his hand at her, the other still fastened to his stomach.

Clap, clap, clap. "Focus, human! You are with the superior beings, now. You must *focus*."

Sasha glowered at Tessie's smug expression.

Charles groaned. That wasn't going to help. When Sasha got angry, she had a harder time controlling the lesser power levels. He'd tried to get her to work in black, because she seemed to mess up less in that power, or even gold, but she was (for good reason) afraid she'd get magic shock. The Boss said they needed to find some better trainers who knew how to work with her; these weren't harnessing what she had to offer. Charles had to agree, and since the Boss was one of the smartest people in the clan, well, he would know. Except, they didn't have anyone. Not without verifying her power with the council. And *that* would mean Stefan would finally have to pick a mate, since them coming out here would serve that purpose as well.

Dicey.

Two more accidents later, and some more aggressive trash talking from the ginger, and it was finally time to call it quits. Charles needed to have a word with James about negative reinforcement...

Sasha needed to give Ginger a fat lip. If this kept up, Charles would have to do it, and picking on a student was expressly forbidden.

"Seriously, Gabe," Sasha was saying as she rubbed his back, "I usually only make a mistake once, so hopefully—I mean, *definitely*—I'll definitely stop hurting you very soon."

Gabe, a soft kid with terrible taste in fashion, shrugged

his thin shoulders. He gave her his attempt at a sultry smile. "It's okay. I'll brave it again to keep being your partner…"

Charles rolled his eyes and yanked Sasha toward the door. "Alright Casanova, let's go."

"Casanova is a guy, nitwit."

"Whatever. You got a hard class next."

"Trying to learn to fight without impaling my partner isn't considered a hard lesson? I think I should use a wooden sword so I can't blast people."

"We have Darla next. I have to participate this time because I don't know *nothing* about chanting and carrying on."

"You don't seem to know *anything*—notice my word choice—about English, either." Sasha's chuckle turned into a groan. "Darla hates me—worse than Ginger. This is gonna suck."

"Yes on both counts."

CHAPTER FOUR

I WALKED INTO THE THIRD STORY ROOM WITH AN AIR OF confidence. Darla might be gorgeous, apparently great at whatever the hell she taught, and promised to the man of my dreams, but she would not get me down.

About eight people sat in chairs around the medium sized room. Darkness loomed outside, sucking the candlelight out of the space. Darla stood in the middle of the room wearing a *chic* red dress that hugged every perfect curve.

"Oh goodie," Darla drawled, "the Boss's pet has graced us with her presence instead of throwing a tantrum and running into the woods. Aren't we so blessedly privileged?"

"Yikes, not pulling any punches, huh?" Charles muttered as he shuffled in beside me.

I took a seat next to a sneering guy a few years older than me. In fact, I appeared to be the youngest in the class. Which meant they were super old.

"Great, let's start where we left off last time, shall we?" Darla turned toward a chair, waved her arms around, and started chanting in a completely foreign language. And not foreign like French, Spanish, or even Latin. No, these weren't real words. It sounded like a bunch of consonants she spat out one by one.

My arms prickled and my chest got warm, the indicator she was working a spell. A similar feeling, though to a much larger degree, also happened when the *Dulca* monster things called to me.

The chair started to bubble, wisps of red gathering and pulling around it, until it kind of...vanished. If you looked right at it you could see bits of it, like right after staring at the sun and having a sun spot obscure it. But if you weren't looking directly at it, you wouldn't notice it there.

It was probably that spell—with a ton more power—that hid the house I lived in. Neat. I really wanted to learn it. Or did it take multiple people to produce?

Darla took her manicured hands out of the air and put them on her hips with a smug nod. "Now, you try."

I stared.

All eight students stood obediently and faced their chairs. Charles followed shortly after.

"I don't know that language," I whispered through half my mouth.

"Did you have a question, *pet?*" Darla's honeyed voice rang out.

I turned slowly, wanting to find a corner to hide in. "Um, I don't know the chants. I'm not sure I'll be able to do this lesson."

Her red lips pulled back into a sickly smile. "Oh, poor baby. You push your *master* to get you in school, but you aren't ready for it." She shrugged, gathering her students' attention like flies to poop, which was exactly how this whole thing smelled. "I guess you'll have to learn on the fly."

Master, huh?

Anger licked at my awareness, surging. I didn't know what the heck she'd just done, but I roughly knew the elements she'd called, and roughly the shape the magic took. Gathering all the ingredients to me, I waved my hands like I thought I'd seen her do, and then gave the thick cloud of red a little push with my palms, nudging it forward gently.

The chair exploded.

Oops.

Wood splinters rocketed out and sprayed the class like bullets. Some students ducked, some crawled away, and one guy, apparently a ninja, did a spider jump, turned it into a flip, and landed on his feet five feet away with his dagger out.

"Care to explain what the *hell* you just did?" Darla screeched.

I faced her with hunched shoulders. "Blew up my chair?"

Her eyes burned into me as the rest of the students drifted out of their sheltered places. "Who taught you to do that?"

Ninja warrior had not tucked away his dagger.

I shrugged, digging my hands into my pockets. My gut twisted. "I thought I was doing what you did..."

"What incantation did you use?" she demanded.

I grimaced. "I didn't. I tried to just download the right elements, swirl them around, and kinda...drape them over the chair..."

"*Download* the right elements? *Swirl* them around?" Her long red nails tapped her crossed arms.

"That's how she thinks of it," Charles helped.

Darla's cool gaze fell on Charles. "Ah yes, the boy wonder. Youngest Watch Commander in a century. And here you are, playing bodyguard to the Boss's pet. How far have we sunk?"

It was Charles's turn to hunch his shoulders. Unlike with the elements or with the sword stuff, Charles wasn't packing a whole lot of confidence in this class. At least we were in it together.

Her gaze speared me again before she turned with a

whoosh, her silky black hair flying. "Pair up. Dog and dog walker, break apart. Let's do some simple spells. How about containment spells? Go."

"That's easy?" Charles mumbled.

I looked around the circle, knowing no one would want to pair with me. I knew I would have to wait until the least liked kid in class had to come shuffling over to pair with the dropout. God, this sucked.

To my horror, Darla noticed the situation, and took matters into her own hands.

"Doggy, pair up with Adnan. Go."

The ninja, fortified with a glare, stalked up to me. Straight, simple movements bespoke an ordinary guy. The fact that he'd just flipped through the air had me intensely nervous. Unlike Gabe, this would be the wrong guy to accidently blast.

"Hi," I squeaked.

He frowned in response.

"I don't know what I'm doing," I warned.

"Then stand there and look pretty. You're apparently great at that."

Ouch. But also, thanks for the compliment.

He held his hands out, palms facing each other. In that strange language, he began chanting. Well, he could've been spitting and hissing for all I knew, but I felt the magic collect and pull, fanning that heat in my chest. Pale red formed between his hands—now green—now red again. He straddled the cusp of power, but I felt more available within him.

"Can you just stop for a sec?" I asked as politely as I could.

His eyes flicked up with a glower. "Why? I'm not going to show you what I'm doing. You should have been here at the beginning of class for that."

I grimaced to prevent myself from retorting like a wiseass.

This guy could kick my ass—bad news with Charles on the other side of the room. "I just want to help."

"How the hell can *you* help?"

Darla hung around near Charles, occasionally petting his muscles or rubbing her fingers across the base of his neck. She was occupied.

"Look, I'm an idiot, yeah, and I largely haven't a clue, but I *do* somehow know how to help others grasp magic. At least, I can with Charles and Master Bert. And, uh, Jessiah." This was not a time for my face to turn red when I mentioned a new crush.

His frown intensified. "What?"

"Just...do it again, and let me put my hand on your skin, that's all."

"Is this some weird attempt at seduction?"

"I can assure you, no."

Frustrated—he didn't seem to have a lot of patience—he shrugged me off with a, "Whatever."

He started again, not allowing me to touch his arm, since that would distract him, so I put it on the side of his stomach. I really tried not to feel his bumpy lateral muscle.

It wasn't me doing the seducing.

"Okay." He concentrated, his intensity blocking off some of his magic flow. Charles did it constantly. Too uptight.

I closed my eyes, focused on his block as I drew in magic, and gradually *pulled,* forcing more magic through to break that block. "Loosen up," I murmured.

He gasped. When I opened my eyes, the magic hovering in front of him, waiting for a command, was deep red.

"What is going on?"

Damn it.

Darla took her hand away from Charles' butt so she could put it on her hip. Her cold gaze leveled us from across the room.

"I was just helping him with his—"

"*You* help someone? You can't even help yourself. Stand in front of him where you're supposed to be so he can put the spell on you."

I trudged to my place, my head lowered, and waited while he summoned that red haze again. It got paler and paler as he worked. "Loosen up. You're struggling to control it. You need to partner with it. Join with it."

Those weren't the right terms, but I was largely learning by feeling it, and I didn't know how else to describe it.

He worked harder, his power level staying in the red, but the intensity of it fluctuating. Finally, after another minute of trying, Darla appeared behind him. "Here, let me help. Next she'll be offering blood for protection to you, too."

She slid her hands down his arms, giving him goose bumps and entwining her fingers in his. "Now, say the words with me."

Her steamy voice entranced him as her breasts squished against his back. Red pulsed between their hands, and then floated over me into a box similar to what Stefan had put me in when trying to protect me. As the box solidified into a translucent, red cage, I touched the side and got the expected shock.

Darla backed away with an evil smile, her hands feeling down the side of Adnan. "That's all for today, class. Charles, you can get your *charge* out of this predicament. I have faith in you."

I'd never gotten so many smirks in my life.

Charles stood in front of me uneasily as the rest of the class filed out merrily. "I have no idea how to make one of these, let alone how to undo one."

"Oh great. I'm trapped. God, she's a bitch!"

Charles nodded, surveying my cage. "Shall I throw a chair at it?"

"I doubt it. How about cutting it with your sword? You have higher magic."

"What about yours? You can do more powerful magic than I can."

My gaze flicked to my dagger, lying forgotten near my hoodie on the other side of the classroom. "I didn't think we'd need it."

Charles sighed and dropped his head, his hands finding purchase on his hips. "Well, what if the blade goes through and cuts you?"

I showed my teeth. "That would be bad. Okay, try your knife, and do it really easy-like."

Charles took out his dagger, waited until it glowed orange, and then gingerly sliced into the box. Sparks lit up the side like a sparkler, but the orange knife parted the red.

"Does it hurt when those sparks touch your skin?" Charles asked, stopping the cutting.

"Yes, it hurts! But keep going. I don't want to be trapped in here forever, and I *don't* want to have to get some human-hating clan member to break me free. I'd look like the clown I am."

"You aren't a clown." He kept cutting, spraying me with burning magic shrapnel. At least, that's what it felt like. "You need to tell the Boss to have her stop. You'll never learn this way."

"No way am I running to my *master*. She'd just find some other way to be a vindictive bitch. At least this way, I know it's coming."

"I guess."

*****

J essiah followed as the human and her bodyguard sauntered into the woods, each with a plate of food. He'd gotten nervous when they didn't emerge from Darla's class, thinking he lost them already, but a half-hour later, when Sasha staggered out with her face and arms full of burn marks, he figured Darla took some sort of petty revenge for the human getting blood from her man.

Jessiah waited patiently near one of the back doors of the mansion, needing to leave time and space between him and his prey so Charles didn't hear him. Despite the immaturity, and Jessiah's taunting, Charles could hold his own better than most guys in the Watch Command. He'd gotten his role guarding the human because he could be relied on and do serious damage when pushed into a corner. Jessiah wanted anything but to push him into a corner.

When the sky began to lighten, and the sun threatened to peek above the horizon, Jessiah left the shadow of the doorway. With soft steps, he rounded the trees and searched for a trail. Not seeing one—the human stepped lighter than he anticipated—Jessiah snuck forward another few paces, listening for voices or sounds of life.

Birds chirped out a good morning. The distant thrush of cars and the city quietly drifted by, but no other sounds of life or nature greeted his ears.

He kept walking, looking for tracks, signs, anything that might direct him to his quandary. After a half-hour of looking, however, he found nothing.

Stopping in the middle of the cluster of trees and brush, he took out his phone and dialed the number. After four rings, a gruff voice answered. "Yeah?"

"I followed them into the woods, but they disappeared." Jessiah turned where he stood and looked out at the trees, squinting into the first rays of the sun.

"She couldn't have just *disappeared*. Where did she go?"

"I don't know. She had that kid Watch Commander with her. He's good at melting into the trees."

"Did they know you followed them?"

"No. They seemed disgruntled from their last class."

The silence hung on the line for a moment. "Fine. Keep tabs on her. Figure out where she goes when she isn't in class. Figure out where she's sleeping. Most importantly, get close to her. Get her to trust you."

"She's the Boss' pet. He's not going to let any harm come to her; and if it does, and he catches me, he'll kill me. I need a guarantee I'll be taken care of."

"You received the packet?"

Jessiah squeezed the phone. A packet of money had awaited him in his room. Tucked into the bills was an organizational chart of the Eastern Territory's guard. His name had appeared in the upper echelon. It was privileged information. Not even the boss had that layout, or the names attached. He was *in*. Thoroughly in. All he had to do was deliver the girl.

Easier said than done, especially with her high-powered friends guarding her.

"Yeah, I got it." He scanned the trees, making sure he was alone.

"Good. Then you know what waits for you. Just deliver the goods, alive and in one piece, and we'll bring you over."

"How'm I supposed to get her out of here without her guards?" He cleared his throat, trying to erase the whine from his voice.

"You're attractive and good with the ladies, I hear. Get creative."

The line clicked off. Jessiah kicked a rock into orbit. How the hell was he going to get her off the grounds?

*****

I walked into the secret room in the middle of the mansion via a door that looked like just another part of the wall. I'd had to use my inner guide to find the secret entrance and open it. As soon as the door clicked shut, pitch black dousing me, I heaved a relieved sigh and let magic fill me. The colors in the wall swirled to life, the gamut of power forming a complex protective ward embedded into the fiber of the mansion.

Alone time. I sighed again, just for good measure.

I'd ditched Charles after dinner—eating "dinner" at five o'clock in the morning still felt wrong—ducked away from the chatty, handsome Jessiah, and bowed my head through the halls of staring eyes. I needed to disappear. To have time to reflect without Charles yapping in my ear. I loved the guy, but after a while, he could be a little much.

I'd been at this magic gig for over two weeks so far. Each class had people who snubbed, sneered at, or ignored me, and each night ended with another torture session from Darla, who hated me more than most people hate the dentist. I was struggling, and that was putting it mildly. Depression from my inability to learn and fit in dragged at me. The only highs I got seemed to be driving fast, but lately that just bordered on recklessness—the forced joy receding shortly after reality seeped back in. I just couldn't get it. I couldn't find my groove.

The desperate thought constantly squeezed me: what if I didn't have a groove? What if I could never fit in? If this had all been a mistake, and I didn't have any way to bounce back, what then?

Forlorn, I walked through the small corridor until it emptied into a medium sized room, the furniture standing out as black spots among the swirls of the rainbow. There wasn't much. A couple couches in the middle of the room, facing each other, a desk in the corner, books, and a rug. I couldn't remember if knickknacks lined the available surfaces, but I suspected not. I wasn't even sure what the room was used for. Nor did I care. It was secret, safe, and empty. Hooray.

The couch welcomed my butt into its embrace, the *kush* loud in the silent room. And there I sat. Staring. Mind empty. Body filled with magic.

I could hold more magic for longer, now. I pushed down the euphoric feeling, took comfort in the vibrant pinging within my skin, and relaxed with it. Jessiah said I shouldn't have magic always at my disposal, that it could burn me out, so I tried to force it away as often as I remembered. The thing was, though, it seeped in naturally. It lingered happily. I just kept forgetting to push it away again.

Today, though, I didn't feel like stressing about it. I wanted to relax. I wanted to forget about school. I actually wanted to hang out with Jared. I no longer had the same feelings for him, but he'd been a friend. He'd been someone to laugh with and hang out with. He'd been a big part of my life, and I still missed his presence.

I hoped he was happy. I hoped he found a good gal to go with his awesome job. He was smart, he would land on his feet if given half a chance. And Stefan had given him just such a chance. I owed Stefan a thanks for that.

Trying to find peace, I blanked my mind and just *felt*. Just let my magic run through me, gushing within me like blood.

A half-hour into my induced state of paralysis, I heard a distant door click, the magic in the walls swirling like ants confronted with a boot. The closing click sounded a minute later, leaving silence in its wake. Another thirty seconds and light bathed my solitude in a soft glow.

Stefan appeared from a corridor on the right, a faded black T-shirt hugging his deliciously defined body. His hair had grown, the tamed messy giving his chiseled face a rogue look—bad boy meets professional model with a trip through the computer for some airbrush. His expressive dark eyes studied my pose as he walked near, noting my slouch and lack of interest in how my limbs spilled over the leather cushions.

He settled on the couch opposite me, eyes still studying.

"Lights." I nodded, not bothering to look around since my head weighed too much. "That makes seeing the details easier."

"Were you afraid someone would find you if you had them on?"

"Hadn't thought about it, actually."

"Then why didn't you turn them on?"

I would have shrugged but my shoulders seemed just as heavy as my head, and therefore, immovable. "Didn't know they existed."

"So you've been sitting in pitch black...why?" His eyes stayed trained on my face.

My eyes stayed trained on his body. Each bump and valley gave me a pang of longing and flare of arousal. It was then I realized another thing I had constantly missed. Him. Seeing his face, talking with him, even for just a moment, feeling his touch. My body constantly reached for his, noticing the absence when he wasn't around. In the same room as him, I didn't feel desperately alone anymore. I didn't feel like something was missing. I wasn't hopeless.

Lot of good it did me. His lady love reminded me of her claim on him nightly.

"I've just been watching the colors swirl around," I said absently. "I wonder if they'd move if no one walked around within the house. But then there is always wind. I wonder if they would swirl in a vacuum? Neat experiment. We should try it."

"What do you mean, swirls?"

"Ugh, you sound like Darla. The magic. In my limited vocabulary, it swirls."

"And you can see this...here? In this room?"

I frowned. "Not as much when the lights are on, but in the pitch dark, yeah. It looks like the northern lights. Which are really cool by the way. I'd love to see them again. Maybe they look different with magic."

Stefan's gaze slid past me, his gaze scanning the walls.

"You can't see that? Or maybe you never tried?" I asked to fill the potentially awkward gap.

He shook his head slowly in a noncommittal response, his gaze returning to me. "You're blocking your link somewhat. You've been doing it often, lately. Why?"

This time I went through the trouble of shrugging. I didn't want to admit that it felt weird flirting with Jessiah when Stefan could peep at my emotions. I had no idea where it might lead with Jessiah, or even if I wanted it to lead anywhere, but I wanted the freedom to make that decision away from prying eyes.

Black eyes stalked me like a lion on the prairie. He probably had some idea where my thoughts had traveled, and judging by the clenched jaw and forced-even breathing, it didn't thrill him.

"Why are you in here?" he asked.

"I'm tired of people. I used to live alone. Now I have Charles around all the time. I barely get time to—" I cut off before I could embarrass myself by saying something intimate, and instead said, "shower."

His eyes caught fire, but he ignored it. "Charles came to find me. You panicked him. He thought you'd run off."

"Sorry about that, but I can't have him following me constantly. It gets overbearing."

He brought his hands to his lap and intertwined his fingers. I got the distinct impression he wanted to go find a chain and secure me to something heavy. It didn't take a genius to know I tested his patience.

"We'll work something out. Please inform him in the future, however. Your ability is known now throughout the clan. Reaching the black power level is still largely a myth, but blowing up chairs, singeing off hair, shooting fire from your dagger, and other such things tend to raise eyebrows. You use red with so much power, it can't stay contained. Even if you never got beyond red, that type of magic is... unusual. Jealous inspiring. Being a human, you are..."

"Not taken seriously? Hated? The butt of practical jokes?"

The corners of his mouth tweaked. "Anomaly fits better, I think. Interesting."

He only thought that because he wasn't in my classes. "Well, my saving grace is my *in*ability. I'm struggling with everything but elements."

His jaw clenched again. "Yes, I am contemplating tutoring."

"Oh, good, *more* of my day down the toilet."

"Night, you mean."

"Semantics."

His lips tweaked up further. He considered me for a minute, that half smile revving up my sexy systems and reminding me of how long it'd been since I'd been touched. Since I'd been kissed. Charles kept pushing me to take part in the house freedoms of sexual expression, but I had this insane fear that people would start making fun of me for my deficiency in sex as well as magic. I also feared that it wouldn't end the dry mouthed *thirst* that I'd had quenched with one *dream* of Stefan. What if it was him, and not just the lack of sex in general?

Still assessing me, his voice lowered when he said, "You never came to report to me. I'd hoped you would."

It took me a moment to figure out what he was referencing. "With an update, you mean?" Charles had mentioned something about that, but the constant badgering from Darla had chased it from both our minds.

Stefan nodded, a relaxed movement, as though this conversation had switched gears, now dribbled in honey. "I haven't seen you in a while. I've missed you."

It took a second for the words to register. He was entirely serious. His eyes had taken on an intimate, soft quality I remembered from when he walked me home.

"Do..."

I stopped with that one word. You couldn't very well ask the guy if he missed other people, too. If this was limited to me, and by it being limited to me, if it meant he viewed me with more importance than a mere subject. How lame would that sound?

His eyebrows quirked, wanting me to finish.

"Um." Suddenly, that weird thing deep inside that felt his pull had to know if he had any semblance of feelings for me. If he, perhaps, felt even a fraction for me like what I felt for him.

"Hmm." But how to phrase it.

Big breath.

"Is, um, that normal? Wanting—I mean, you know, missing a...minion. Or whatever?"

I was a dynamite linguist.

A smile flickered. "Open the link."

With magic already occupying my body like blood, I merely had to swish away the muffle on our connection, and there he was, pouring into me. His impassive face contrasted the emotions warring in his body. Warmth glowed through him, tingly anticipation at being in the same room with me, and the desire to stay in my presence. Arousal flamed, but was overshadowed by his belief in me; in his confidence that I was doing well, and would continue to make him proud. He was showing how much he supported me, and what it meant to sit calmly, relaxed, in the same room without worry of his status or position. With me, he got to be a man, not a leader.

He liked me!

God, I was a dumb girl, but I could barely talk! The electricity in my body surged to enormous heights. It suddenly occurred to me that we were alone, in a secret place that no one else would find, at the end of the night. The way he was looking at me, too, implied his willingness to whatever I wanted; going our separate ways, talking, snuggling, other...things.

My heart started hammering, suddenly nervous.

"Don't be nervous," he whispered. His smile flickered. "I am at your mercy."

"Does, ah..." I cleared my throat, sweat coating my forehead. "Does anyone know you're in here?" The tightness in my groin was reaching up through my body and squeezing my brain.

"No one. Everyone thinks I've turned in except for Charles. There's no way I can taint your reputation from this meeting."

I stared at him for a second, wondering if he knew what I was asking. Wondering if I would finally get to do this; to satisfy this soul clenching *need*. Being bold, I rose slowly, my desired solitude long forgotten. His eyes watched me aloofly, waiting to see what I would do. Watching, completely still, as I crossed the four feet between us. Standing beside his legs, my knees butting against the couch, I hesitated.

Now what?

Still he waited, fire in his eyes, heat pumping through the link. He wanted me. I wanted him.

Oh good god I was nervous.

With a deep breath, I eased a leg over his lap, settling myself with my groin over his, his hardness pushing against me. His hands gripped my legs as his face fell. The link soaked through with guilt.

"Wait, Sasha, I have to tell you something." His eyes lost some of their passion. "The night I gave you blood—the second time—I...invaded your personal space."

I leaned closer, heat infusing the space between our mouths. "Mm."

"I had you drink from my neck, but then you got aroused, and..." He cut off, his lips squeezing together in a hard line. Releasing a breath, he finished. "I took advantage of you."

I blinked. His expression held remorse to accentuate the guilt from the link.

"It wasn't a dream," I whispered, strangely confused. That was why I only remembered glimpses of his face; why most of the experience was sensations. Exquisite, earth moving sensations.

"I should be pissed off, and if I was still with Jared, I would be. But...I remember asking for more. Did you not hear that? Was that not out loud?"

"I did, but you were on your death bed. It was beyond stupid. And irresponsible. And...creepy."

"I creeped you out?" I couldn't help my rigidness.

He shook his head in frustration. "I made love to a sleeping girl with a fever without first getting her permission. No, you weren't the creepy one."

I smiled away my insecurity, running my fingers along his raven stubble. Maybe it was creepy, but I didn't care. I remembered the feelings—more than just physical. I remembered the closeness that I thought could only be a

dream since it felt so completely *natural*. I wanted
that again.

His face lost expression immediately, his hands tightening
on my hips, as I moved back in, my breath ruffling his hair.
My lips glanced his, then more pressure. I licked his bottom
lip, asking admittance. He opened to me, licking my open
mouth, teasing, chasing my tongue with his.

I slid my hands up his muscular arms, feeling the strength
in his biceps and the brawn of his shoulders, before letting
my palm settle at the edge of his jaw.

I backed off enough to speak, "Does it feel good when
someone takes your blood? I've often heard Charles mention
it as the most intimate of things. He doesn't do it lightly."

"Yes," he whispered. His hands felt around my body to
cup my butt. "Would you like to take more of mine?"

"I was thinking the opposite. Maybe you should take mine
this time? Even the score. I want to feel what it's like."

His mouth dipped to my throat, my head falling back to
allow him access. My breath came in fast pants as his lips
skimmed my pulse. His kiss was gentle, but he did not bite. "I
can't take yours."

"Why? What did I do wrong? Too much garlic in
my diet?"

He chuckled, his tongue flicking out and licking the base
of my neck. "We'll just say, I don't want to mess with...anyway."

I made an unhappy sound before claiming his lips again,
frustrated with the amount of fabric between us. I sat up and
unbuttoned my shirt, exposing my breasts slowly, my cleavage
holding his attention. My blouse fell from my shoulders. My
bra quickly followed.

His hand caressed down my chest, cupping a breast in his
palm, rubbing my nipple with his coarse thumb. Pleasure
erupted in my core, tied directly to my breast. When he bent

down and took it into his mouth, sucking and teasing, I couldn't believe how good it felt.

He backed off quickly, shedding his T-shirt, and sitting back, two hands now on me. I lowered my hands to his shoulders, feeling the grooves of muscle with my fingertips. I traced down his chest, running my palms over his defined pecs, down his smooth skin to his rippled abs. Surveying, I ran my hands over his strong arms, his tattoos seeming to wave under my fingers.

"Why the tattoos?" I murmured, running my hands back up slowly, letting the anticipation build.

"They're runes. Spells. They have many uses. For one, they aid in delivering...power. Our hands and arms become weapons, like our swords. Another reason is they gather the darkness, helping us camouflage. Also, they help send magic airborne, like when I wrapped that protective spell around you. We can easily fortify an object with magic, like our swords, or like the walls, but it takes a certain amount of power for magic to travel. Runes, in a set pattern, make that easier."

"But I can throw magic without runes. Often when trying to do something normal."

His hands slid up my back, making me shiver pleasantly. "Mages have more versatility, they have the power and ability to allow magic a life of its own. Even they require tattoos, usually. You are rare. In so many ways."

He leaned forward, touching his lips to the base of my neck, then kissing upward to my jaw. His hands crept toward the front of me, to my lower stomach. I felt my top button released with a tiny jerk. My eyes closed as my zipper lowered.

He stood, a mountain moving, taking me with him. Setting me down, his hulking body in front of me, his head lowered to mine, he gently pushed my pants down my thighs, my undies hitch-hiking a ride to the floor.

Another zipper ripped down, pants discarded. Stefan stood naked in front of me, his giant member erect and bobbing, freed. I had remembered his size from what I thought was my dream.

It still shocked me.

I inhaled a deep breath as he backed away and sat down, that massive erection half daunting. At least to a woman of my limited experience.

"At your pace," he whispered. Understanding and support filtered through our link. His eyes, soft, waited patiently for me.

I grinned. "It fit once. And felt really, *really* good, if memory serves."

"Too good, maybe." I barely heard his voice.

"But...protection?"

He shook his head. "We don't have the same issues with diseases as humans. Something with our blood eats diseases—maybe its nature taking it easy on us since we have a hard enough time procreating."

I stared at him for a long moment, making sure it wasn't one of those things a man says to get out of wearing protection. The link radiated honesty, though. And it made sense.

He interrupted my pondering with, "But we can get humans pregnant."

My brow furrowed. "You can? Even though we're different species?"

He half smiled, connecting his warm lips with my chest. "We are different, but not fundamentally diverse enough to prevent the merging of DNA. There are other problems, like watering down magic, and acting like a lottery for each species to inherent gifts, such as they are, but..."

I waved it away before he could tell me we wouldn't be

marrying and having children, anyway. I couldn't have reality messing this up. I didn't want the impracticality of *happily ever after* messing up the glory of *right this moment*. I wanted my dreams of him to last a little while longer.

Plus, I stayed on the pill after Jared for regularity. Problem solved.

Trying to find my breath through my constricted chest, I straddled him again, flattening his manhood with my body, and touched my lips to his. I felt his lips curl before he answered, passion unfurling between us. I got lost in the kiss, sucked into a void where the world fell away around us. He licked and tasted my mouth expertly, teasing but wanting. I clung on to his body, his tight arms around me.

I slid my body forward, then back, rubbing along his shaft. When we were good and slick, I raised a fraction, his arms around me lightly shaking. His tip crested my folds, having me nearly weeping with the anticipation. I sat, slowly, his girth invading my body, stretching me to the point of pain.

I pulled up, trying to work him in. His hands flew out to the sides, straight along the couch back, and clutched at the cushions. Intense concentration took over his face.

Back down again, filling me. More stretching, the sweet torture having my eyes fluttering. It felt so good—I couldn't remember anything, ever, feeling this damn *good!*

"Oh god, Sasha—." Stefan's whole body flexed as his eyes squeezed tight, preventing himself from thrusting upward by sheer strength of will.

My heart sank. I wish I knew how to do this better—he was just so big. It hurt to force it, but I could tell he couldn't handle the slow torture of working it in. "I'm sorry, I'm trying to—"

Stefan's eyes snapped open. His arms crushed me to his chest as he laughed. "Don't be sorry! I haven't felt this good in…a long time. Keep going. Don't worry about me. If all torture felt this good, I would never have another worry as long as I lived."

He kissed me sweetly, his hands shaking on my hips.

I let out a relieved sigh as my body started its downward descent, once again reveling in that sweet torture. He was right about that—it felt almost unbearably good. I wanted to laugh and cry with each plunge, working in a little farther each time. I was oh-so-graciously full, every sensitive spot sparking and pinging around my body. His hips pushed up, forcing just a tiny bit more in, about three-fourths inside. His arms flew to the sides again, apparently trying to keep from grabbing me and jamming me down.

I bounced twice more, sighing with each plunge. Nearly there, now, barely stretching around his girth.

"Oh fuck." He panted. "I might…can't…*oh*—" He shuddered, my body filled in a different way.

I stared at him, shocked and wide-eyed. I'd been atop Mt. Premature many a time, I just hadn't thought it would be with him.

Ready for the "that's okay" smile, I put my palms on his chest to push away, only to have his hands grab my wrists and his eyes open again, hooded.

A lazy smile slid up his face. "It's probably better that way," he said easily, relaxed.

He secured my hands around his neck before his palms found and started kneading my breasts. "I haven't been with anyone since…well, you. Full speed ahead."

"You can keep going?"

He gave me a scoffing eyebrow quirk. "You don't think I'd leave you on the edge do you? What kind of a male does that?"

"From what I've heard, a normal one."

His grin turned smug. "Exactly. Proceed."

Half laughing to myself, I sat down, not paying as much attention as I should have been. A dull ache stopped me, my hands clutching his shoulders like claws, telling him to stop even though I was the one in control.

"Here, let the creep take over," he whispered, clutching me to his body with one hand and turning us over so he was on top of me on the couch. "I recently had experience in these matters."

His lips attached to mine, deep and needy. One hand enclosed my breast, his fingers flicking my nipple, causing me to squirm. His other hand paid attention to the top of my sex where I felt things the hardest. A pleasure-filled squirm turned into a full scale buck, thrusting my hips up to meet his. His manhood dug deep, embedded to the hilt, our ends rubbing together.

"Oh!" I sighed, the dull ache only lingering a moment, and unable to compete with his ministrations.

He began moving slowly, working my body with those clever fingers, building me. Each muscle started to flex, then release, flex, release, and release again. His hard shaft moved into me, gaining speed. Shivers wracked me, leaving more intensity in their wake. My body sweating, his slick as well, he worked into me, deeper and harder, faster.

My legs squeezed his thighs, my arms clutched his shoulders, my mouth kissed his neck. The pleasure condensed in on itself, localizing in my groin, tightening. Everything tightening. My body getting dense, blasts silently bursting all over my body in muffled detonations, hinting toward that final event. Tighter still, muscles shaking, Stefan groaning, his face against mine. The world sparkling with color so intense, I could barely stand it. Everything pulled down, winding up, then—

"Oh, Stefan!" I cried, my body convulsing under him with such intensity, I could barely breathe. Jackhammers of pleasure echoed through my limbs, infusing me with euphoria as the vibration subsided. I had so many endorphins, I wanted to rocket off the couch. I was so relaxed, I didn't even want to move enough to turn my head, tingles of lingering sensation creeping throughout my body.

Ho-ly hell.

All this time, I had no idea what sex was really supposed to be. What a true orgasm could really feel like. It was... I was...

I'd never be the same.

Stefan lay over me, limp, his face buried in my neck.

"Please tell me you are satisfied, because it might take a miracle to get me hard again," Stefan mumbled into my neck.

"No. Good. Wish this was a bed." And I did. How the hell would I get back to my room? I didn't want to ruin this feeling by walking.

Then I didn't have to. Stefan climbed off, wobbling, grinning, and scooped me up.

"Clothes?" I asked sleepily, curling around his upper body and laying my head between his neck and shoulder.

"It's late. Nobody will notice."

"Nobody will notice two naked people wandering through the halls?"

"We'll take the hidden tunnels to the far-eastern door and exit directly outside; but then, no, they won't notice. Plus, no one is out there."

"Right, I forgot which house I lived in."

"My house."

"Yes, sweetie, that's right. This is your house." She patted his arm.

Stefan chuckled. A cozy walk later in Stefan's arms, I felt the bow of magic as we passed through the wards of my hidden residence.

"Hey Boss, whatcha got there?" I vaguely heard Charles moving around.

"I found your charge."

"You certainly did. You also *serviced* my charge. Thank the merciful gods. Maybe now she won't be so wound up."

"Please be careful how you address my pet."

"Not funny." My voice didn't have much conviction. My body was too busy trying to shut down.

As Stefan laid me down, he said, "Sleep tight. Have pleasant dreams of me."

"Cad."

And he was gone, shutting my door with a soft click.

CHAPTER FIVE

"Run!"

A giant mouth made by petals swooped down, trying to catch me. I scrambled back, terrified, my magic winked off as I stared at my fifteen-foot-high creation. The goal was to *coerce* a natural element to grow. I created a plant beast.

Charles dashed forward, glowing sword in hand. He ripped me out of the way, hurling me back to the center of the classroom. He slashed at the monster, swiping half a flowered mouth off, only to curse when it grew back.

"Sasha, what the hell did you do?" Charles yelled, dodging a lovely smelling chomp.

"Made the plant grow!" I screamed back, my own dagger in hand, glowing a bright orange.

"You weren't supposed to—" he feinted and struck, slashing off a giant, reaching leaf, "give it an agenda!"

"Maybe they naturally have agendas." I sprinted to his side, bobbing and weaving, looking for an opening. I'd made some great strides at stabbing things. I was quick.

I felt my arm yanked, hurtled back behind Charles again, this time by Adnan, his sword glowing a pale blue.

"Don't fire magic at it, it might make it bigger," Adnan yelled.

Yeah, I was also great at setting magical fire to my opponent accidentally. Gabe said it actually felt good half the time. He was such a trooper.

Adnan, the ninja, darted with such speed, I stood in awe. He whipped around, almost dancing, and then retreating before the curly green shoots of the plant could capture his legs. Unfortunately, his blade didn't do a dang thing. I'd created the beast with a strong red power and he was only using blue, two steps down; his eagerness suffocating him.

"Relax, Adnan! Open up to it."

I focused on the elements in the room, feeling the currents, sampling the percentages. There was always a healthy amount of air, of course, but the other elements were often disguised within the life around them. A humid day held good doses of water, so did pipes and toilets, and other household areas. Fire existed in electricity, in sparks. Earth, of course, was all around, but often so far beneath me or removed, I couldn't work with it easily. I felt it was my greatest weakness, as did Charles, but Jessiah didn't seem perturbed, so I didn't fret too heavily.

I felt everyone's magic around me, but honed in on Adnan. Like someone with asthma, he wasn't drawing enough because his receptors were tightened.

I sucked in a big draw, connecting with his flare of magic and billowing it higher. I did it to Charles, too, since I was taking the time. Sweet essence pumped into me, fanning the other boys higher as their magic tried to flirt and play with mine.

"Good times, Sasha," Charles said, darting in between angry green stalks to slash at a thick green stem. "Don't do that when you actually have to...work magic...though. You'll be weaker."

"Yes, professor obvious. I figured that."

Adnan's blade glowed orangey-red. He was in business.

He dodged in, jumped with a neat flip, and landed on the other side of the evil plant. He stabbed it through a petal, and then hacked off a vine. Charles met it from the front, slashing again at the stem.

In another few minutes, it was over. My cute but violent flower lay in a puddle of plant parts, the room looking like a weed whacker went wild on a garden. Charles stood in the middle of the melee, sweaty and loving it, his smoky eyes bright. He flashed Adnan a triumphant smile, striding over to shake the younger man's hand.

"With fighting like that, the Boss would welcome you in the Command with open arms," Charles boomed, swagger fit for a prince who'd just slain a dragon.

Adnan returned the compliment with a sheepish grin, his eyes briefly flicking to me. He'd always had the ability in movement, just not the power to back it up. Apparently he realized I wasn't such a useless jerk after all. *Hah!*

Well, maybe the jerk part was right enough, but still.

A slow, jarring clap echoed through the room. Darla stood against the far wall near the door, a mocking expression on her face. "Yes-oh-yes, let the little dog create a magical nightmare to show off, then let her big tough *bodyguard* take it down. Quite a spectacle. Maybe they were thinking no one would notice how weak they are in spells and chanting, hmm? Well, maybe we should—"

The door swung open, thankfully halting Darla. She always had creative ways to put me on display. Jessiah stood framed in the doorway, his wide shoulders making his upper body look like a triangle. My heart fluttered weakly, wishing Jessiah had the same effect on me Stefan did. But then, Jessiah wasn't attached to the slinky, long-haired beauty next to the door, with her perfect breasts nearly falling out of her tube top, and her long, slender body draped just so—a weak flutter was better than nothing.

Raising my chin and pushing down my insecurity, while muffling the link with Stefan—hoping he wouldn't notice if I didn't cut it off completely—I tried to keep a hopeful expression from my face. I'd been getting closer and closer to Jessiah over the past few weeks, learning heaps, but also just having someone to talk to who wasn't hell-bent on keeping me prisoner. He was kind and thoughtful, often giving me a flower and a smile when we met for the lesson.

And right now, he counted as a savior, because I knew Darla wouldn't make fun of a student in front of another teacher. She was vindictive, not stupid.

"I was told your class would be finishing about now?" Jessiah asked with a gleam in his eyes, touching Darla with just enough sex appeal—which he had in droves—to get his way, but not so much as to distract him from what he'd come to procure. *Me!*

I nearly gushed like a twelve-year-old!

"Just finished, yes. The human created a giant plant that had to be destroyed, cutting my teaching time in half."

"Ah." Jessiah's eyes twinkled as they beheld me. "She excels in creativity." He winked.

"Hmm." Darla's eyes roamed Jessiah's body, lingering on his arms and stopping for a brief moment between his legs. Her gaze returned to his face, heat kindling.

"I'll just be escorting her out, if you don't mind?" Jessiah stepped toward me and away from Darla.

That move right there, which made him the only person besides Charles who would say no to the tramp, endeared him to me. At a spiteful nod, I took his warm hand and let him lead me through the door, Charles hot on my heels.

"Wait, *you*, I want that mess cleaned up." Darla stopped Charles with a flaying stare.

"That's not my job. *She* is my job."

A red haze blocked the door, that protection spell Charles still couldn't figure out how to work was locking him in. As I hustled away with Jessiah, I heard her harsh laughter.

"Do we need to wait?" Jessiah hesitated.

I tugged him along. "Nah. He's around *constantly*. I doubt anything's waiting in the woods to accost us. And if it is, I can blow up a plant to attack it. Or us."

He laughed merrily, tucking my arm around his.

"So, what do I owe the pleasure?" I asked as we sauntered toward the trees, the night silky and warm on my face.

The soft moonlight caught his beautiful blue eyes as they beheld me, soft heat infusing them. "I never get to talk to you. It seems like you've always got somewhere to be or something to do."

"Or Charles nudging me away?"

Jessiah grinned, threading his fingers between mine to hold my hand. "He doesn't trust me with his women."

I laughed because it was so true, even though I wasn't Charles's woman. "He is a *tiny* bit jealous, yes. I've noticed."

A powerful surge blasted through the link, Stefan extremely uncomfortable about something. Given that he was always irritated in some way about his duties, this was par for the course. I stopped the link altogether, wanting a freaking second to myself to figure out this attraction to Jessiah. No, I couldn't even feel a fraction for him what I did for Stefan, but I wanted to see if this interest was returned—healthy and reciprocal without an arranged agreement with other women. It tipped the balance.

"You've come a long way in your elements. Do you have any other help?"

"Just you. I like your teaching style. I am a hands-on learner, so how you show me helps." I blushed a little. Granted, sometimes his hands wandered a little too close to personal areas, but he always apologized with that devilish smile, the scoundrel side of him making me laugh.

As if thinking along the same lines as I did, he smiled. "Hmm. So, where do you stay while you're here? I haven't seen you around the mansion after light."

We walked through a canopy of trees, heading deep into the woods. The leaves draped across the sky, hiding the approaching dawn. The last traces of night called to me, the silken feel of darkness reaching for my body and caressing my senses.

"I'm tucked away," I answered, leaning against his shoulder as we walked. "Where do you stay?"

He paused next to a tree, directing my back toward the bark. His eyes looked down into mine, the woods still and quiet in the pocket of time when night animals tucked into their beds and the day animals got the urge to wake up. His hands lowered to my hips.

"On the first floor of the main house with all the other minions," he said in a husky voice.

My hands traveled up his arms, smaller than Stefan's. He didn't have the medieval tattoos to make him seem exotic and wild, either. Or the giant width of shoulder from fighting and surviving in the world, keeping his people safe and protected.

With effort, I ignored all that, glancing back to his face. He was handsome, surely, but not devastatingly so. His eyes didn't hold the same wicked intelligence, or the same soul-touching depth. My heart didn't pound, or lurch, or even flutter. My stomach didn't tingle or fill with butterflies.

Damn it!

Jessiah leaned in, his mouth brushing mine softly. A pang of guilt rocked me, unexpected. This wasn't wrong logically, but my soul didn't know that. This man wasn't the one I truly wanted. He wasn't my ground; my other half.

That man was promised to someone ten times prettier

with a long list of accolades. And I'd thought I'd always been lucky? *Yeah right.*

I pushed back, moving my head to the side to escape the kiss. Regardless of Stefan's attachment, I didn't want Jessiah. At least not right then. I wasn't ready.

"What's wrong?" he asked, his head still bowed to mine.

"I should probably get back."

His eyes delved into mine, making me shiver in a way I wasn't expecting. Before I could identify the weird thrill of— apprehension? Fear?—a rustling caught my attention. Adnan stepped through the foliage.

"Sasha, sorry to interrupt, but do you have a minute?" Adnan nodded to Jessiah in acknowledgement.

For a race of people who had sex while carrying on conversations, I wasn't sure why this intrusion surprised me. I was equally confused as to why it relieved me as well.

"What's up?" I stepped away from Jessiah smoothly, using Adnan as an excuse to head toward dinner.

"I wondered..." he hesitated, his gaze flicking back to Jessiah, who apparently did not intend to follow. I hoped he wasn't mad. "You helped me today—thanks—and I wondered if you would continue to help me if I helped you in turn? Maybe if I taught you some sword and chanting, if maybe you'd work with me on keeping my power open when I fight? Without that, I can't get into the Watch Command, which is the one thing I've been training for my whole life."

Ah, the dramatics of youth. Still, this sounded like a sweet deal! Maybe I'd even get a friend out of it. "Sure."

We got within sight of the mansion. I scanned the back wall, looking for my pissed off bodyguard. "Where's Charles?"

"He got worried when you took off, so he sent me after you."

"Why didn't he come after me himself?"

"He went to look for the Boss, I think."

"Oh great, he's telling on me, that butt-head!" I shook my head as we walked through the door. I might as well just use the time to my advantage.

To that end, I snagged some dinner from the dining hall and headed straight for my room. Eat, shower, *alone* time. I still had Stefan on the brain.

*****

"I had her, where were you?" Jessiah barked into the phone. "It's not easy to get her alone!"

A growl filled the line. "You think I can get people to you in five minutes? That I can mobilize the right equipment from a random text you send? You have to plan it out! You need to coordinate this."

Jessiah kicked at the ground. It had been a huge stroke of luck getting Sasha without that fool Charles. Although, it seemed that Charles had trouble breaking protective spells.

"I have an idea. Be ready tomorrow at dawn. I'll text you the exact location and time. Be in position before I arrive. I'll trap her bodyguard and hand wrap her to be taken. Just be there."

"You are dangerously close to overstepping your bounds." The voice on the other end paused, menace nearly crawling through the line and into Jessiah's head. He'd forgotten the type of men he was dealing with. The dangerous nature of the type of men he dealt with.

"Sorry, sir."

"Have her ready. I'll organize the pick-up."

"Yes, sir."

Jessiah dropped the phone and took a deep breath.

Warning tingles filled his whole body. He wondered if he was really making the right decision.

That organizational chart flipped in his head.

Steeling his determination, he headed back to the mansion to finalize his plans.

CHAPTER SIX

"Boss, I need to talk to you."

Stefan finished reading the document Jameson had handed him and faced Charles, a bad feeling taking over the pit of this stomach. "What is it?"

"Sasha took off with Jessiah after Darla's class."

Stefan waited for more. When it didn't come, he dropped his hands to his sides so he didn't shake the other man. "Why didn't you go after her?"

"Because that bi—uh, lovely future-mate of yours slapped a defensive shield in my face, *knowing* I have trouble with those, and allowed her to escape."

Stefan's head tilted slowly. "Darla prevented you from going after your charge? By a *defensive* shield? Your power grossly tops hers, not to mention the help of the runes. Are you so thick you can't learn to break a simple spell in a month?"

"Boss, it's damn hard to learn when that stupi—when the teacher won't actually *teach*. At least I basically know the structure of the chants, but Sasha doesn't even know that much. She spends the whole class blowing things up, shooting them out of the room, or, like today, creating monsters for us to take down. Though, I have to say, that giant plant monster was actually—"

Stefan hardened his gaze, cutting off the other man immediately. "Are you telling me that Darla is withholding information? Why didn't you come to me with this?"

Charles shrunk into his shirt. "Sasha didn't want to tattle because she, quite rightly, figured Darla would just get vindictive."

"So, you're telling me—a wasted month later—that Sasha has learned nothing?"

"Well, she's learned plenty, and some things will probably be extremely useful, but nothing that's on the class agenda."

Stefan took great pains to control his facial expressions. Darla had become the biggest nuisance of his life. She'd been pestering him for blood constantly, and if not that, a formal mating, and if not that, sex. He'd never had a firm fondness for her, but he'd always been able to tolerate her, especially when she spread her legs. Now the thought turned him off entirely.

"How close has Sasha gotten to Jessiah?" Stefan stepped away to the corner of the library and threw up a voice diffusor, his tattoos glowing so faintly, no one would be the wiser.

Charles stuck his hands in his pocket. "He's trying every trick he's got, and she's buying it about a fourth of the time. He's a sniveling little jerk, but he does have game; I have to give him that. I don't trust him, though. He's uncommonly frustrated...like he has an ulterior motive. He's trying to get her to trust him rather than just getting in her pants, but he is nowhere near sincere. That's not normal."

Charles stared at Stefan, trying to do the mental deduction in his head. He thought with his dick often enough, but making sense of that with the head was still beyond him.

He tried again. "Okay, like, a guy that waits for sex either really likes the chick and will endure the blue balls to make her smile, or he wants something. Jessiah doesn't really like her. I've pulled his angle a million times. He's after what's between her legs, and something else..."

Charles' voice dropped away, his eyes widening at whatever he saw on Stefan's face.

Stefan realized he'd stopped breathing. He smoothed over his face and unclenched his fists. "So you think he wants something, and she's buying into him at least part of the time?"

"Like I said, he's got game. Plus, she misses that Jared kid, and she's lonely. I probably would've had a chance if I waited. I mean, she'd probably buy into anyone who was nice to her. Want me to beat him up? It'd be my pleasure..."

"Where is she now?"

"I sent Adnan to get her. You gotta keep your eye on him, Boss. Adnan, I mean. That kid can *fight!* If he can keep his magic up, he's a shoe-in."

Stefan, voice low, growled out his next words. "Instead of going yourself, you sent a half-trained child to retrieve my— to bring back Sasha?"

Charles' eyes snapped shut and his easy-go-lucky attitude dried up. He'd just realized how serious this conversation was, and he was late to the party. In a rush, he said, "It's only Jessiah and they were headed out to the woods. I came to get you while he went and got her. I got a text from Adnan—she got food a short while ago and headed off to her room. She thinks I talk too much for some reason, so half the time she tries to ditch me. Kind of mean, actually, but she's okay."

"What makes you think she won't hook up with Jessiah knowing you're gone?"

Charles shrugged, his eyebrows dipping in confusion. "She knows not to reveal her sleeping whereabouts..."

"It doesn't mean he won't have her in his."

Stefan couldn't help his rough voice. It killed him to imagine another man touching her. Stefan had no claim on her. He was spoken for; his duty clearly mapped out to choose a mate. When a person became leader, he had to give up certain things. His path was set, and Sasha needed to find someone else and be happy.

A vase shattered against the wall. Everyone in the room turned to him with shock or fear written plainly on their face. He probably shouldn't have thrown it.

"What do I do, Boss?" Charles asked quietly from five feet away, not daring to take a step closer.

"If he is using her, keep him away from her. *Break him* if you have to. I will not see her hurt." He swung a fierce gaze across the spectators, daring anyone to mutter the term *pet*. He'd snap them in half, no guilt or remorse in his wake.

As Charles took off, Stefan set his sights on Darla and started walking. She not only hindered Sasha and Charles with her pettiness, she hindered his whole clan. She would be dealt with.

He found her in the library, naked and riding on top of Thaos, a younger man with pale orange power. As her hips swiveled over him, having him moaning and rolling his eyes back in his head, she sucked at his wrist, drawing deep, having used her body to steal what she could of his power.

This is what he would be mated to. *This* is who Fate had mapped out for him; the best option of the bunch.

"Darla, get up."

Startled, the woman's gaze shifted to his eyes, widening as she beheld him. She dropped Thaos' wrist and stood, leaving a moaning man with a lulling head in her wake.

"Hello, come to join in?" She sauntered up to him in a silky glide, all hip and breast, covered in another male's sweat.

Stefan pushed her away with a grimace. "What is this I hear about you failing to teach your new students?"

She laughed sardonically, her smile brittle and bitter. "Oh, is that why you finally seek me out? For your precious human *pet?* Well, what did you expect, Stefan? She has about as much talent as any human, and less finesse than most. She only wields red. You are wasting your time with her—I only wanted to help you realize that."

"If I hear of this again, you will be disbanded. Do I make myself clear? Monday you will have a shadow. I think it's time I checked on your ability as a professional—"

Arousal washed through the link, filling him up, making his balls tingle.

Earlier, when she'd been with Jessiah, she'd muffled it, trying to disguise what she was up to, obviously making him pay attention to it more heavily. She thought she was sneaky, which usually made him laugh because it meant she'd blown something up or otherwise made a huge mess Charles would undoubtedly have to kill. This time, he waited on the edge, wondering what feelings would shine through in the end.

Arousal was the opposite of what he'd hoped. And being that she'd let the muffling slip, she was in the height of passion.

A shot of fear coursed through him, fusing his jaw shut and making his hands fists. Being that fear was not an emotion he allowed, rage quickly took its place. Turning abruptly, he was out of the room, striding across the mansion and out the back door with fast, determined strides. He could not suffer her to be touched by another male, his duty be damned; especially not one seeking to use her—aiming to crush her under his agenda.

*****

C harles dried himself off with a towel, passing by Sasha's closed door. Her rinsed plates had been left in the sink when he'd walked in, and the shower had been used and returned to heightened organization. She'd prepared for a quiet night in, and even though he hated going to sleep without a night cap, he knew better than to barge in. The last time he did, she'd blasted him with that weird magic throwing thing of hers. It hurt, and she'd only used a pale purple.

It was pretty cool she could fluctuate the amount of power she used, though. He'd tried that and only given himself a headache.

As he walked down the hall, he felt the strange surge that said someone was entering the ward. He turned back to the door, his towel clutched in his hand and the rest of him air-drying, wondering if the Boss planned on a night cap of his own with the sensual little human. Man, what he wouldn't give for a crack at her. She'd be a wild ride, he had no doubt. The way she—

The door burst open, scattering his thoughts. The Boss barged through, his shoulders taking up the width of the frame, his eyes ready to rip a body limb from limb. Women often said he had a face like an angel, if that angel hadn't shaved in a day and road a Harley. In Charles's opinion, if that angel also decided to go on a killing spree with the intention of taking out half the world. His body brimmed with battle rage, each substantial slab of muscle flexing. Eyes on fire, tattoos alight with his powerful magic, he bore down on Charles.

"Where is she?"

"I-in her r-room. I swear!"

"Did you touch her?"

"No. Gods, n-no." Charles put his hands up in surrender,

begging to die quickly. "My dick shrivels just thinking of it. I don't want to go anywhere n-near her." After today, that would be a solid truth.

"Who's in there with her?" His voice rumbled like a guillotine sliding toward a neck.

Charles's eyes got wider, if that were possible. "N-no one. I don't think. I'm pretty su—"

"Move."

Charles dove out of the way, wanting to be anywhere but in the warpath of the Boss when violence called. If there was someone in there, he wouldn't be in one piece for long.

*****

Stefan kicked open the door, the room gloomy where the dark, heavy curtains tried to block out the rising sun. Sasha lay on the bed, the duvet just showing two peaks of knees with a valley in between, her legs spread. At his entrance, she jumped, her head snapping to the door with giant eyes.

Brain not registering logic anymore, his animal instincts of possession completely taking over, Stefan walked at her, eyes on who might be between her thighs. A certain untrustworthy asshole that was about to die between her thighs.

He bent down and ripped away her duvet, throwing it across the room. Her thighs were spread wide, her crotch covered by white, lacy panties, the middle wet. Her hands, braced to either side of her in surprise, had two glistening fingers.

His eyes met hers. He saw the heat and felt the pulse through the link. She'd been thinking of him.

A new awareness claimed him.

Mine.

He reached down to her, ripping away her panties in one yank. His clothes fell off a second later, so fast it was like he wasn't wearing any. Not wasting any time, he settled between her thighs, pinning her to the mattress possessively.

Mine.

He claimed her lips, filling her mouth as she opened to him. She tasted of spices, like mulled wine, and smelled like the forest after a spring rain. He pushed himself into her body, hot and fast, digging in to the hilt. She moaned, opening to him, body and soul, offering herself up.

Raw, animalistic lust overcame him, his body pushing harder. He trapped her beneath him, dominating her completely. Deeper he strove, taking delight in her moans and pants.

It wasn't enough. He wanted more. He wanted all of her.

Mate!

With a growl, he bit, teeth cutting through the soft skin of her throat just over the pulse. She sucked in a breath at the sharp pain, fingers digging into his back. With his first deep suck, she mewed, melting like hot wax. Power filled him like a current, magic blossoming deep in his chest in a way he'd never experienced. Her magic was so pure, like tapping directly into the source. His tattoos started to glow a burnished gold. With each swallow, it got lighter and lighter until they glowed a gold crusted white. She filled him.

His body slapped against hers, feeling the power well up, her legs around his hips, her arms hugging him close. He released more of that secretion into her, feeling it in the core of his being. Wanting the marking complete, forever.

"Take my blood." His voice was deep and gruff, primal.

He snatched the dagger on the nightstand and made a small cut in the skin on his neck. Lowering back down, she took to him eagerly, her hips rising up to meet each of his thrusts. Her soft lips fastened on his skin, the first draw causing him to suck in a sweet breath of glory, her scent infusing the sensations. Their power swirled, mixing together and fusing their essence—one soul split into two bodies.

"Oh *Stefan,*" she sighed, blasting the link wide open. A love so deep, it consumed him and poured through. It spilled into all the dark and shut-up places; filling up all the haunts and sadness in his life; healing it with her. His chest burned and his limbs tingled, more magic pumping into his body than he'd ever experienced. A sweet elation took his breath away, her essence riding the wave like a surfer. She was imparting her own mark, one just as permanent, and just as driven by a place without thought.

"Harder, Stefan. *Harder.*"

The world disappearing, all he could focus on was her. Her beautiful face, eyes lit up in wonder. The feel of her body, smooth and delicate, spurring him deeper, taking him higher. Of her magic, pure and sweet, encasing them in a bubble of pure delight.

"Submit to me," Stefan commanded softly, his voice gruff and primal. He stopped, not allowing her to move until she did.

A languid smile lit up her face. "Back to that again, are we? I remember you saying that in the alley the first time we were alone." She paused for a minute, her husky voice hiding the nervousness. "You first."

It sounded as if she didn't expect him to dive in with her. "Forever. You will want for nothing. I will make sure of it."

"I've always been yours, Stefan; you know that."

He closed his eyes in relief. "Yes."

With renewed determination, he crashed into her, the pressure growing, taking over. Tighter and tighter it coiled, the sensations almost unbearable.

"Oh, Stefan..." Her fingers clutched at him and her body tensed.

Stefan licked at her neck, opening the quickly-healed cut, waiting for that right moment. A few more strokes into her tight body and he was ready, fissure lines working through his very fiber.

Her moaning got higher, almost there. Almost...

As she neared that edge, balancing on the cliff, he sucked in, the pull tugging deep in her body.

"*Oh!*" Her eyes fluttered and she shuddered, her insides squeezing Stefan so tight, he nearly blacked out.

He blasted his seed into her a second later, pushing her into the mattress, bellowing with the glory of the orgasm. Their combined magic blossomed and flowered, the whole room drenched in a feeling so intoxicating, it felt like they hovered, weightless, only knowing the feeling of each other's body.

He kissed her deeply, his body fractured, wanting her to collect the pieces and fit them back together however she wished.

When they stopped panting, lying exhausted in the quiet room, she said, "You forgot to yell *surprise* when you barged in earlier." Her laughing voice dripped with awe and completion.

"I saved it for this moment." He shifted to the side, leaving himself inside her but removing some of his weight. "I figured I'd give you the best orgasm you've ever had, and then say it...Surprise."

"You're under the impression that was the best orgasm I've ever had? Not overly full of yourself, are you?"

He laughed. "Confident, there's a difference. And yes, that was the best. I figure if I've never had better, and I've had way more experience in these matters, then it must rock your world, too."

"I haven't experimented much. I hadn't realized that fact until the people in this house opened my eyes."

Stefan laughed. "Well, now you have me to experiment on."

Her arms, resting on his back, still wanting that closeness, momentarily tightened. "How long can you stay?"

His eyes drooped, consciousness fleeting. He was so damn relaxed, yet the magic pumped within his blood. He'd never felt this truly alive before, especially while also never feeling this complete and utterly satisfied.

The woman did nothing but complicate his life, but for all that, he would never walk away. Not from her. He'd have to make some decisions, but no one else was getting her. She was his. End of story. The question was, how did he both keep her and his duty? How did he compromise to keep her near?

He only had two months to figure it out before the Regional got there, but it would have to wait another turn of the sun because he was in no mood for thinking at the moment.

Answering her question, he said, "All day. If you'll have me."

"Hmm. In that case, can you move off my leg a fraction so it doesn't fall asleep before I do?"

He kissed her cheek. "Of course. We'll need to speak about what I just did, but it has to wait. I can barely keep my eyes open."

"Hmm." She was asleep before he'd finished adjusting.

Yup, she was gonna play hell on his life, but there was nothing for it now. The decision had been made in that first second his eyes had touched hers under the streetlight those few months ago. It was amazing he'd resisted this long.

Fate was such a tricky bitch.

CHAPTER SEVEN

I CAME AWAKE WITH A SOFT KISS BRUSHING MY LIPS. I threw my arms around the culprit—a large, muscled hunk—and smiled good morning...or evening, rather. He wore the same clothes as when he'd barged in, but seemed more relaxed. The stress lines on his face had softened, making him almost hard to look at he was so danged handsome. I said so.

He smiled his flawless smile, making me blink in wonder at the rest of the transformation into super-hot.

"To think, I've hated having women in my bed. Turns out, I just hated having the wrong ones," he said quietly with soft eyes.

Warmth filled my midsection. I smiled like a fool.

"I have to go to work," he said tenderly. "I'll see you close to dawn."

"You're going to spend the night with me again? How'd I get so lucky? Or are you attempting to take a pet...which you very well know that—"

He claimed her lips, his kiss deep and passionate. "We still need to talk about what I did. You might not think you're lucky by the end of the night."

I tilted my head, surveying his suddenly serious face, and then falling into those dark eyes. "Cryptic."

He straightened up, tall and broad, a man of strength and power. Who would've thought he could be so gentle. "I'll talk to you later, love. Leave that link open, I want you present always."

"Bossy." I turned and glanced at the clock. Time to get up. Damn.

"Sasha."

I waved him away and climbed out of bed. "I'm going to give you a firm maybe on that one."

He growled and slapped my butt. "Talk to you later." Before he walked out the ruined door, he paused. "Oh, and... I'll fix this." His head nodded to the broken hinges.

"By the morning."

"Morning-ish. Also, be easy on Charles. I think I scared him."

"When you were freaking out for no discernible reason, you mean?"

"There was a discernible reason—"

"Which you will explain."

"—that I don't intend to apologize for—"

"But you will, anyway."

"—but, yes, when my...dander was up last night. He got the brunt of it."

"Well, I got the good part. Although, maybe taking it easy for the next couple days might be in order."

His eyes took on a liquid heat, arousal flooding through the link. He almost started back to me, every muscle on his sizable frame taut, but he held firm. Shaking his head that little bit, he grinned. "Note taken. I bet I can make it even better with a longer build-up."

"Hmm, yes please."

Committing his smiling face to memory for my spank bank, I headed for the shower.

After I had finished getting ready, I glanced around for Charles. Usually, he was in annoying me by now, unable to keep from talking for longer than a few hours at a time. On the way out the door, I finally found him, huddled naked behind a plant in the corner by the door, the thin green leaves shaking, doing a poor job of hiding his whole body.

I stopped, staring down at him. "Hey. What-ah...whatchya doin'?"

"Oh nothing much. Just crouching here behind this plant in a puddle of urine. I'm naked though, so I dried quick. Spot of luck on that score."

I struggled to keep a smile from my face. "How long have you been there?"

"Oh, just since the Boss came barreling through in a battle rage. Thought he'd kill me. Then thought he'd kill whoever was with you. Then thought he might kill you accidentally because you tried to save someone, all while I hid in the bush like a bitch. Not my finest moment, Sasha, but it's been a while since I saw that crazy male in a rage. Took me by surprise."

I stepped behind the plant and hauled him up. "You didn't really piss yourself, did you?"

"Yeah. Please don't tell anyone. There's a reason that man has been the leader so long. He's got great logic, sure, great leadership, great loyalty to his people—but if all that fails, he freaks the fuck out. He scares the shit outta me. Yuck, and you still smell like him."

"I do?" I smelled myself. I'd taken a shower, so I had no idea how that was possible, but these guys had subatomic noses, so who knew. "Anyway, we're gonna be late. Hurry up."

"How are you so chipper this morning? I expected

screams of terror when he beat your door down, not a blast of magic and a loud orgasm."

My body zinged with remembrance. My knees went wobbly and I stumbled into Charles' door. I hadn't been scared for one minute. I felt him coming, his rage as a means to hide a deep fear. I didn't know what he had been afraid of, but when he stood, silhouetted in my door, my heart stopped.

In his battle rage, as Charles called it, he'd been magnificent. Like a raging Viking of old, his powerful body flexed from head to toe, his thick slabs of muscle on display in the best of ways. His eyes had been on fire, hair wild, his purpose honed and sharpened.

Seeing him like that triggered the thrill I'd always had; the side of me that needed fast cars and rose to meet danger with a knife and a snarl. I couldn't help but hold my arms wide, waiting for him to rush in and take me, dragging me in and under, losing the world as we raged toward each other until climax.

And we'd done just that. I'd willingly taken blood, somehow not grossed out in the least. I'd also given it, engaging in feelings that I couldn't even understand, let alone explain. The sensations had been so deep, reaching the center of me, and then tickling.

And the magic...

I sighed as Charles quickly hopped in the shower. Usually, I half-raged trying to stop the flow of magic into my body, then had to organize and spread it out so I didn't feel weirdly lopsided. It always felt great, joyous, and exhilarating, but it took work. Stefan's added power presence had smoothed all that out. Balanced it. Made drawing easy and storing effortless.

"Quit daydreaming, we gotta go," Charles said as he passed by with a towel wrapped around his middle.

"What's up with the coverage?" I asked as I followed him

to his room. "I'm not used to seeing you glistening without a naked show of some sort—"

The door closed in my face.

Taken aback, I tried the handle, only to find it locked.

"Are you mad at me?" I called through the wood.

The door swung open a moment later, Charles grim and clothed, his eyes downcast. "No, but I never want to see you naked again, I never want to think that you saw me naked, and I do not want any sort of arousal passing through my brain where it concerns you."

Still without meeting my eyes, he squeezed past as if I had a contagious virus.

"What the hell did I do to you?" I asked in outrage, following him. "Because I left with Jessiah? Did you get in trouble or something? And what does that have to do with your love of nudity?"

Charles spun on me, making me shrink back. "That crazy fucking male you're sleeping with nearly tore my head off thinking I'd touched you. I do not intend..."

Charles trailed away, his expression changing to one of disbelief. "He marked you."

My hand flew to my neck. "Yeah, we exchanged blood. Is that weird?"

"No—" Charles leaned forward to enunciate his words very carefully. "He...marked...you."

I glanced down at my body, checked over my arms, and then turned my puzzled expression back to Charles. "How? Where?"

"Did he not explain what that meant?"

I shook my head, still lost to confusion. "He said he had to talk to me about what he did. I figured it had to do with him breaking down my door, and making my roommate piss himself and then sleep in a bush."

"I didn't sleep. I was afraid he'd come out." Charles shook

his head. "Not important. A male hasn't marked anyone in... decades. He was probably embarrassed or he would've told you."

"Why? What does it mean? Is it bad?"

Charles held the door and yanked his head for me to go through. "Back in the day, when you staked your whole life on one female, you'd mark her. You'd declare yourself as the defender to her and her offspring, to the death. You basically said you were her department store; whatever she could possibly need or want, it was your job to provide. Darla wants that from him like nobody's business."

My heart fluttered. Stefan had given me something he wouldn't give his intended. That another man hadn't given a woman in a great many years. I didn't understand fully what it meant, but that alone made me feel special. It made me feel... important to him. Treasured.

Charles went on. "It's a great risk to him, though. If anyone goes after you, it's a challenge to him directly. As a leader, he will be forced to answer the challenge—all challenges—or he loses his title. Not to mention his girl and his pride, obviously."

"So, basically, the mark is to ward everyone away from me with the implied warning 'or else.'"

Charles nodded.

"And...he's promised to another."

Charles nodded again, but this time, with a grimace. "We stopped marking because times changed. We're extremely promiscuous as a culture—it wouldn't be fair to limit that."

"So, after you mate, you still screw whomever?"

"'Course. Though less as you age, obviously. But yeah, mating is really meant to provide stability for offspring and protect the family. You might have noticed—we are a fairly violent race."

"But I haven't seen any families around here..."

"We wouldn't be so stupid as to have pregnant females and children hanging around the city where Trek and his idiots are roaming free. Families with children are in our lands in the woods or more suburban settlements."

I took a deep breath. On one hand, it was a little unbelievable that Stefan would care for me that much. As Charles said, based on his peoples' culture, this was way huger than marriage. That gave me a dramatic pause.

On the other hand, he just cut off my ability to find someone else within this species. When he got mated, I would have a giant, permanent road block to my moving on. I couldn't get pissed at him and breakup because I'd still be tagged as his. I'd be cast off and alone, it would be him or nobody.

"Humans can't tell, right? This is just limited to your race?" I inquired to Charles as we neared the main house. I slowed for obvious reasons. Yes, I needed food, but I got suddenly worried how people would perceive me. Something told me I'd get more stares than usual.

"No, humans wouldn't know. If it goes pear shaped with him, you can always snag a human."

That helped lessen the blockage in my chest. Realistically, he was my other half. Being together last night felt so instinctive. I wouldn't get that with someone else. Anyone else. Still, fail-safes were good.

Then something occurred to me.

"If I want to cause him no end of grief, and possible death, all I have to do is seduce someone?"

Charles thought about it a second. "Huh. Yeah. I guess you kind of have the upper hand on that one. If anyone would touch you. He's the top of the food chain, so..."

"They're men. Men are dumb when they get turned on."

"Good point. Please don't try to seduce me."

"Why? Afraid you'll give in?"

"Obviously. Thank the gods you're not a vindictive bitch."

"That you know of."

"Oh no, I've catalogued your bitch side. You are an explosive, wild, unpredictable bitch, but if I avoid the triggers, I'm good."

"You still manage to surprise me."

"As long as I don't turn you on, I don't care."

We entered the dining hall. Five steps in and people started to notice the difference in me. Wide eyes turned to stare, sticking to me as if I was a ghost. By the time I had breakfast on my plate, the whole place was silent.

"This is awkward," Charles whispered, his head down.

"Yes, Charles, this *is* awkward. Thank you for pointing it out."

A gasp went around the fifty or so spectators. I glanced up to find Stefan entering the room, three people at his back. Face stern, his eyes locked on me, his body heading over in a calm, measured pace. People's eyes darted back and forth between us, ample entertainment.

When he reached me, he put his hand on my cheek. Then, surprising me, leaned down to kiss my lips. "Good evening, beautiful. I felt your embarrassment, so I figured you were here. I'm trying to lessen the...discomfiture."

"Not helping," Charles muttered, making himself as small as possible. He wouldn't look at Stefan.

"Did you come to me last night with the intention to mark me?" I asked quietly, allowing Stefan to lead me to a table in the middle of the dining hall. He was openly staking his claim, which helped cement that the mark had to do with his feelings for me, and not his professional interest.

"No, I did not. I wasn't thinking at all, actually. Nothing had been planned out. We can talk about it more later, though, without prying ears and judgment. I try to keep personal business behind closed doors. For now, I want to enjoy eating with you. Sitting with you. What's your first class today?"

"Elements. Then weaponry—I'm getting a sword today. Most of the class is terrified. Then charms and spells. Why don't you have to chant when you do a charm?"

"More advanced and powerful magic users can *will* the magic without having to form it with words." He shook his head, his eyes never looking away from my face. The world could be on fire, but as he sat there, speaking with me, he wouldn't have noticed. I had his sole attention. "You have the weekend off from charms and spells. Go back Monday. I'm sending someone to shadow Darla."

"Ordinarily I would say 'butt out,' but in light of this mark thing you gave me, I think I'll nod to that. I don't feel like dying today."

"You don't have to worry about that. My job has always been to protect you."

"Yeah, okay, that gives me a soft spot and all, but this is a little heavy for morning chatter."

"Evening chatter, I think you mean." His dark eyes sparkled, but in his role, he didn't show humor, so he kept his face impassive.

"Right. Okay, I'm off. Thanks for strangely sitting at the table, staring at me and not eating, but I gotta go."

He shook his head, a smile almost breaking free that time. "I'll see you in the morning. Unless you need something. Call me or come to me anytime for any reason."

"So, if I called you up, pulled you out of a meeting, and asked that you provide me with a teddy bear as big as my body with a black and gold bowtie around its neck—you know, symbolizing our combined power—you would comply?"

He stared at me a minute, still ignoring the world around him, probably trying to process the strange woman he'd tied himself to. Finally he said, "My duty, in that case, would be to ensure your mental welfare hadn't taken a shit."

"Potty mouth!" I glanced around us, noticing that people had restarted their daily lives, but constantly glanced at us, wondering what would happen next. "Can I touch you?"

He answered by putting a hand gently to my jaw and giving me a light kiss on the lips. "Will you dine with me in the morning? Every morning? As our last stop before bed?"

I winked, trying to stay casual, but did a happy dance on the inside. "Maybe."

The very corners of his lips tugged as he shook his head. As he walked away, I swore I heard, "Complicating..." before his words got lost in the noise.

"Well, at least now he's in a good mood." Charles put his plate in the dirty dish tray. "And he got us off the hook with Darla. Thank the gods for their mercy! I'll be half dead by then and really wasn't looking forward to going."

"How many gods do you guys worship?"

Charles did a double take as we made our way to Jessiah. "Talk about one-eighty?"

"No, you mentioned gods. That didn't come out of nowhere!"

Charles ignored me, staring at his sexual nemesis, who waited under a tree monitoring our approach with an uncustomary grim face. "Why's he dressed all commando, I wonder?"

Jessiah's eyes widened when we got closer, probably noticing whatever mark he could see or smell that I couldn't. His face went white as he stepped forward. "Hi. I wanted to get deeper into the woods today to surround ourselves with dirt. Follow me."

Charles looked around with his customary loathing. "We're surrounded by dirt right here. That's what the brown stuff is called."

I elbowed him, following after Jessiah's quick steps. "You would do better if you kept an open mind."

"I would do better with better teaching. Where the hell are we going?"

"Given the nature of Sasha's mark," Jessiah answered even though the question had been mostly rhetorical, "I figure it's best if we wander even farther. People will catch a whiff and come to investigate otherwise."

"How good is the smell you people have?" I wondered quietly.

Charles looked behind them. "Not so good that we have to go all the way—"

A surge of magic cut Charles off and had my bones vibrating. My limbs banded together with glowing orange light and my draw from the elements snapped. As I fell to the ground, stunned and completely bewildered, I noticed Charles encased in a long box of the same orangey glow. A protective spell. The kind he had a helluva time breaking loose from.

Fuck.

Eight pairs of boots crunched the earth, stepping toward us in a surrounding circle. By my head stood one more, the pair I recognized. *Traitor!*

"Sasha, use your magic!" Charles commanded in a rage-filled, gruff voice I'd never heard before.

"I can't—the source is cut off somehow. What's going on?" I cried.

"Get her up. Leave him, let's go." The speaker used a honeyed voice I almost recognized.

"Reach for that source, Sasha. You can do it! Break through," Charles yelled.

"You want me to leave him, sir?" another speaker asked. "Won't he tell the others?"

"He won't be able to get out of that spell. Not without the counter, and Jessiah assures me he doesn't know it. Plus, he's hard to kill—I don't want men dying trying to manage it when he inevitably gets that one chance. We leave him. We don't need him."

A blindfold went around my head before I could see any faces but one. Jessiah's. Satisfied and smirking. He'd sold me out.

*****

Stefan sat with his top council, going over the territory breaches and logistics, when a shot of pure panic bled through the link. He sat up straight, focusing on that feeling. Panic, pain, fear, and betrayal, intensifying.

"Boss?"

Stefan held up his hand to Jameson, silencing the other man. "Something is..." He stood slowly, the feelings going on and on, not changing to embarrassment like normal when Sasha made a mistake in class. The fear escalated, if anything.

A blast of pain, then emptiness. Sasha had lost consciousness through some sort of trauma.

"She's been taken!"

Fear gripped him in an icy hand, squeezing his heart and making it difficult to breathe. Counting to ten, he let the bonfire of rage warm him back up. Whoever dared take his female would die a gruesome death.

"Sasha?" Jameson asked, rising. His eyes stared at Stefan's arms. "It's true then, she can wield black. And you've taken her blood."

Stefan glanced down quickly, mind still whirling. His tattoos were white with only a faint gold, his power stepped up a notch because of the power he'd ingested from Sasha. It felt good. He felt invincible. Except that someone had clutched him by the vitals by taking her.

"We need all the intel we've got." Stefan rushed out of the room, needing his leather and weapons. Every army man in the room flocked to his side. "She'll be taken to Trek. He'll probably want to bleed her, among other things." White-hot rage filled his body, clenching his jaw. If anyone so much as laid a hand on her...

"Can't she break free? If she is that powerful?" Sturg asked, a battle-honed man with a great many years under his belt. He specialized in the sword and attack spells.

"She is untrained. Largely untrained. Darla did next to nothing and Charles didn't trust..." Jessiah was the instructor for elements. That's where Sasha should be right now. With Jessiah. That maggot.

"Get people out to the woods," Stefan barked, forging into the equipment room. "Jessiah organized this, I'd bet anything. Find his trail. It'll lead to her. Organize the troops and the magic throwers. They'll take her to a secure location, especially once they identify the mark on her. We go in hard and hot, killing anyone we run into."

A chorus of battle-hardened men chirped, "Yes, Boss."

Today was a good day to spill some blood.

CHAPTER EIGHT

It felt like a jackhammer banged around in my head as I came to. My surroundings swam into focus—two groups of men standing around in a modern room decorated in gobs of money. Unlike the mansion, which did classic refinement in its sleep, this place tried to keep up with the times, having no idea what that actually meant. Strange looking chairs and couches, some without backs, many without arms, crouched around the space, uncomfortable looking and spindly. Loud paintings hung on the walls, blasting the eye with colors a four-year-old wouldn't put together. The rug, some sort of new age shag thing, didn't match with one piece of décor.

It looked like someone took acid then decorated this room.

"Ah, she is awake. Wonderful."

That voice...where did I know it?

A man swam into focus, tall and lithe. He approached me with a graceful, aristocratic saunter.

Andris, the man who had tried to take Jared in the past. Lovely.

"And, we meet again." His gaze scanned my body. "And, not hurt too much, I trust? My minions can be rather rough, but we did need you unconscious."

I stood in the middle of the room, hands and legs still clamped to my body with an orange glow. In the corner rested a cage, human height. It didn't take a genius to figure out where I was going next.

"You can resist my pheromones. Interesting. I had heard that, of course, but didn't believe it. Such a rare trait for a human. And a magic wielder, however terrible...my, my, Stefan does unearth the modern marvels, does he not?"

"Is this a monologue, or did you expect some input?" I asked in a gruff voice, strained with the magic roped around my neck. It attached me to a pole. Through the link, I felt Stefan, fear eating away at him like acid, but trying to mask the vulnerability with boiled rage and vengeance. He knew, then.

"It's just that, without accepting the pheromones, you might not have a wonderful time of it. I'm not sure what the White Mage plans to do with you, but you are too pretty to waste."

"A dose of foreshadowing from an excelled storyteller. What a treat. Say, listen, how about you transfer me over to that cage now. My feet hurt. I want to sit down."

A smile erupted onto his face. "What fun. A human with spirit. The screamers do get tiring. The White Mage will be along shortly."

"Goodie." I slouched against the magic, letting the pole take my weight. It wasn't the most comfortable of arrangements, but it was better than some things I could think of. And given that this situation was so far messed up, fear could potentially drag me under and cause Stefan unneeded stress (which would road block his effectiveness at a rescue), I had to focus on only the most positive of circumstances.

A cage and sitting down was it. My life had really taken a turn from cramming for a mid-term.

As people murmured around me, I randomly thought of my rape whistle. While it wouldn't help right at the moment, it had been a trusty sidekick to my independent battles thus far. I felt a little underprepared without it.

Loving support pushed through the link, forcing a tear from my eye. Stefan knew I was awake and he used our shared connection to speak to me, to remind me I wasn't alone.

Steeling my courage, I focused on that damn blockage cutting off my magic. If I could just reach my magic, I could at least get free. Then, with an arsenal of pointy objects and my illustrious butt pucker, I could turn this whole place into a giant, angry garden while I made a run for it. I didn't know many useful spells, but I did know some damaging, hard to clean-up ones. Plus, I could make almost anything explode.

I tried to suck in magic through that block. It felt like trying to suck a thick milkshake through a tiny straw. I tried to punch at it, shake it, suck harder. Nothing.

Just then, the double door at the far end of the spacious room swung open. A progression walked through—a short, thin man at the head wearing a white, velvet cape. His pale eyes, almost anemic, swept the room, landing on me and sticking. His neck glowed like a flashlight, the skin a solid mass of colorless tattoos so as not to mar the brilliant, pure light. He didn't look like much, except his magic, but those eyes had my stomach crawling.

"You've been caught," he said as he approached. His voice was flimsy and squeaky.

"Jesus, your genetics didn't do you any favors, did they?" I blurted, past manners.

My legs hurt, I was a prisoner, and being nice wouldn't grant me any favors. Not with this lot. Best I could hope for was triggering anger that might help me push past that blockage.

He regarded me as a mathematician regards an equation. "You reek of that upstart. Disgusting." He took a large step back.

"He has marked her," Andris helped.

"Can it be removed? Or can I supplant it with my own? I might like to keep her for a while, put her with my maiden stock," the White Mage fired back, still analyzing me.

"It cannot be removed, but I'm not sure if you can supplant it. You can try, but you would have to give her your blood."

The White Mage recoiled. "That just won't do. Has she proven her power level?"

"Jessiah has said—"

"Who?" The White Mage looked back at his second in charge, his hands crossing over his shiny, satin coated chest.

"The boy who delivered her. He said the rumor is that she can wield black, but he has only ever seen her use red."

"Black?" The White Mage laughed. "That is a myth, my dear friend. I have been seeking to push into black since I learned I held white. I've bled countless bodies dry, one after the other, and I only reach the color you see. If she could wield a power that strong, she would not be held like she is. No, that ingrate Boss of theirs most likely spread that rumor, trying to frighten us. Still, red power and a pretty face...we can use her. I just don't know why we went to all this trouble to get her."

Andris's eyebrows rumbled in confusion. "The Boss has marked her, which is reason enough."

He was doubting himself, he must be. I'd used black on him when he was fighting Stefan, bands of magic making him drop his sword, but it'd all been so hectic. In the face of the White Mage's disdain, and the fact this whole group of people thought black magic was one big myth, especially from a human, Andris wasn't so sure. It was a small stroke of luck. I hoped.

The White Mage thought a second. "Yes, I supposed it is. No doubt he will try to save her. He's always been a little too...*noble*. Too bad he will never find her until it is too late. Or have they figured out this stronghold?"

"We've been using it for months, and continue to do so—no, he doesn't know this place exists. Your magic obscures it."

"Good, yes. I had wondered. A huge draw to keep it updated, but worth it, I think."

"What are your plans for her?"

The White Mage's gaze slid down my body. He shrugged, "Bleed her like the others, I suppose. She's no good for fun with that awful stench of his. Keep her here until I'm ready for her. I want to make a few more *Dulcha,* then I'll use her to refill."

"And what of Jessiah? He has been promised a high position for delivering her."

The White Mage turned back. "Who?"

"The boy we spoke of."

"Oh." Arms still crossed over his chest, the White Mage tapped his chin. "Is he any good?"

"Fare with the elements, but no real use other than knowledge."

"Power?"

"Not much."

Those pale eyes stared into Andris, all the calm calculation flaying away, showing a ruthless killer with complete disregard for human life. I shivered as he said, "He has no power, no real skill, and you waste my time asking what to do with him? Get rid of him, skin him and drain his blood; I don't care."

"I'll give him to the men, sir. He's pretty."

"Fine, whatever. Take care of it."

"Yes, sir."

As soon as the White Mage left, hazel eyes turned to me. "I need some information."

"No surprise there," I muttered in a dry voice.

"I need to know the layout of the mansion. The layout of the grounds. How the Boss operates. Small trifles like that. Give me that information, and I won't let the men rape you mercilessly waiting for the White Mage to be ready for you."

"Oh, how sweet of you. And to think, I thought you were an asshole this whole time. Well, bad news. I'm lost in that place most of the time, so you're asking the wrong girl."

He stalked closer, his body brimming with malice. "You want me to dole you out, then, is that it? My guards aren't generally easy with the enemy."

I leaned my pounding head against the pole. "You apparently think I'm an idiot without a shred of observation. Or maybe you just deal with men too much. That mage fellow wears a cape, for cripes-sakes. A white, velvet cape. You think he's going to play with the leftovers of a bunch of minions? Plus, and I think you'll agree with me here, I'm slightly more valuable than a ragdoll plaything. As you probably remember..."

Andris stared at me quietly.

"Let me clarify: I'm calling your bluff," I enunciated. "Your move."

"Your mouth will get you in trouble, little girl. It's not wise to taunt me."

"I'm tied to a pole, in a secret place Stefan doesn't know about, awaiting some loser in a cape to suck all my blood out. I'm already in trouble. But seriously, I can't believe that guy wears a freaking cape! He reads way too many comics."

Andris slapped my face, the sound ringing out through

the room. As my head painfully ripped to the side, he said, "Put her in the cage."

*****

"Boss!" Charles limped into the Planning Room, his body fried from head to toe. He'd had to cut his way out of that damn box, searing himself halfway to the burn ward to do it, but damned if he would stay out of this fight. They'd taken Sasha out from under his nose. He'd rip their whole world down to get her back.

The Boss turned at his voice, dark eyes assessing the quickly-scabbing carnage. "If you would've held on, I sent trackers to find your location."

"I didn't know that, nor did I plan to hold on. Andris was in charge of the extraction."

The Boss nodded thoughtfully. "I figured as much. We don't know where they've taken her. I know their general area, but it's within our territory."

"How do you know her general area?"

"She has always acted as a sort of homing beacon to me. Since the blood link, it is now more precise. The problem is, we don't know anything about this location—the defense, the number of guards, nothing."

"Send me in first. I'll figure it out and report back."

Stefan shook his head. "We don't have the time. We'll go in strong and cut our way through. We'll have to think on the fly."

"No problem." Charles hefted his sword. "I'm good at thinking on the fly. I'll go suit up."

"One more thing—"

Charles turned back to the still figure, a rock among crashing waves, immovable and solid despite what he personally faced.

"Get Jonas. I'll need him for this."

Calling in the big guns. Although, Charles wasn't sure it was the best move. The Boss had always trusted the man, but he was often the only one. Plus, Jonas hated Sasha. Hated her. It would be a bad day to find out the Boss's trust had been misplaced...

*****

An explosion rocked my cage, deep and distant. Everyone in the room—only moments before lounging and waiting like robots on sleep mode—hustled to the doors, peering out. Another explosion on the opposite side of what seemed like a large campus. Through the link poured determination and cold vengeance.

Stefan had shown up.

A surge of sweet gratitude and deep rooted love welled up in me. I could've cried. I wanted to, in fact, but a part of me said to stay strong. Stay vigilant. To help Stefan with the rescue as much as possible, however possible.

An outpouring of men burst through the double doors—my dear friend, Andris, with some stern-eyed fighting men, nearly head-to-toe covered in glowing orange and red tattoos. They headed straight for me, Andris' eyes burning a hazel fury.

"How did they find us?" he yelled, ripping the door to my prison open and yanking me out by my hair.

Pain flared as I squinted up at him. "You forgot to paint

the outside in camouflage? Let me guess, the building is white..."

He shook me and flung me to the ground. Another crowd stormed through the doors, holding a scantily clad man fighting for his life. Guards dropped him to the floor, aiming three well-placed kicks to keep the man down.

My heart wrenched. It was Jessiah. His wild eyes gaped out of a black-and-blue face, fear running rampant. This is what happened when you sold yourself to an enemy for a bartering chip that could be taken from you. Once you proved yourself a traitor, with nothing to sit on after the deal was done, you made yourself expendable. I shouldn't have felt compassion for what he'd done to me, but it was hard to look at him without it.

"How did they find us?" Andris repeated, staring at Jessiah now.

"I-I don't know. The Boss has been trying to find this place for months. He's never been able to."

"Unless he sent in a spy..." Andris turned back to me. "Did you let yourself get taken, little girl? Are you smarter than you seem?"

"Smarter than I seem? Hell, I'd have to be pretty dumb to end up in this situation, hmm? Which makes me wonder how dumb exactly you think I am..."

"A smart mouth at a time like this? You will lose your cool when the White Mage—ah, here he is now."

Cape billowing behind him, the runt of the litter came marching in, his face a terrible mask of fury. His eyes found Jessiah first, hard and cold, staring down at the once-attractive man with that shrewd gaze. "You've been holding out on us. How did he find this place? Only you or the girl could have told him. You are the only traitor of the two, so..."

The White Mage's tattoos flared, bright white. Jessiah started to scream, a shrill plea for help as his body convulsed on the floor. I could almost feel the magic as it brushed against the blockage, seeking admittance to my body. I scrabbled at it, my warning butt tingle telling me danger was in the room.

"Tell me what I wish to know, and I will spare you," the White Mage said softly, bending down toward a panting Jessiah.

"I do-don't know. I only spoke to my contact about all this. That was all."

"Did you alert the girl before you ambushed her?"

"No! I swear! She wouldn't have followed me if she'd known. Nor her bodyguard."

White flared again, a palpable thing. The room must have been drenched in magic, the power so intense, I could almost taste it. When the pain washed away, Jessiah lay, crying and broken, spilling secrets no one cared to hear. His body bent strangely and blood vessels had burst in his eyes. It seemed like he'd been electrocuted to within an inch of his life.

"Finish him. He's of no use, as I suspected." The White Mage straightened up and looked at me, someone else dragging a sobbing Jessiah away.

Terrible fear washed over me as tears dripped down my face. I backed against the wall, shaking and crying, never having seen anything so absolutely violent in all my life.

"What do you know that you aren't telling me?" The White Mage stalked closer, cornering a trapped animal.

"Your cape is ridiculous and your face is something not even a mother could love."

If army men were the gasping type, the room would've been stuffed with inhales. I knew, though, that anger made people do stupid things. Rash things. The White Mage would kill me—obviously—so I could only hope I pissed him off enough to do it quickly, or make some other mistake that freed me. Yes, I was grasping at straws, but I couldn't see any other way.

"He found this place only after I took you and that sniveling wretch into our walls. The missing link exists with one of you, and I am betting on you. You have only a fraction of time to tell me before I feed you to my *Dulcha*."

I pushed and yanked at that damn block, trying like hell to get it out of the way. My inner compass on all things danger said to stall. To keep pushing at him. To prompt some sort of response.

I was not having a good day.

"Then what?" I glanced around, noting exits, planning an unlikely escape, feeling Stefan coming, but slowly. So, so slowly.

"Then they will suck the magic out of you, of course. They need to feed, to replenish their magic supply. Humans with power as high as yours don't come around all that often. You'd be a great treat."

Another blast, shaking the compound. Pain bled through the link; Stefan had taken a hit.

I forced down the desperation. I had to get the show on the road.

"Bring 'em on in. You won't get anything out of me—"

Agony.

Blinding, consuming, soul wrenching agony.

My mind detached and drifted away, shutting off the ripping, tearing, heart-stopping pain. Like pure fire burning every inch of my body while electricity fried my thoughts and peeled away my skin. My hair pulled out one by one. My teeth pulled without drugs. Needles jabbed in my eyes and under my finger nails.

When I distantly realized my body stopped hurting, I floated back into my head gradually, embodying the residual pain enough to laugh like a madman. Blood oozed out of my mouth. I must have bitten my tongue.

"Fuck you, Trek!" I spat, a long red smear on the wood floor. "Bring your useless *Dulcha*. Before I die, I will kill you."

My mind drifted away again, closing off into a chamber without pain. A place I knew I couldn't exist for long without my body dying. But at the minute, my body was dying anyway, might as well cut off the pain.

CHAPTER NINE

S<small>TEFAN STABBED A MAN THROUGH THE STOMACH</small>, <small>THEN</small> swung his sword around and took off his head. Blood sprayed his body.

The door to the warehouse loomed just up ahead. Their guards were falling one-by-one, unable to counter the excellent fighting of Stefan and his men. At the opposite end of the long, white, rectangular building, Jameson led another crew, trying to divide and force their way in, as well.

Stefan knew very well that heavy magic awaited them inside.

Shock and fear bled through the link thus far, which was fine. It meant Sasha lived. But he'd just felt a body-consuming pain; so much so, he staggered, narrowly missing a dagger to the face. They tortured her, most likely. It meant he had no time.

"Hurry!" Stefan screamed, charging forth. "Give it all you have. We must get through!"

He ran forward, blade swinging, cleaving and felling anyone in his path. Slash to the chest, another to the gut, one more to cut off an arm, and he pushed closer still.

A magical blast pulsed out from the warehouse, vibrating Stefan's core. Sasha's magical influence in his body reared up, soaking in that blast and ingesting it. He felt high from giddiness. If he had to face off with Trek, he might just win. After taking Sasha's blood, he was still a small step behind in power, but he'd trained harder. He had more finesse. Knew more tricks and attacks.

If Sasha lay unconscious, what he had would have to be enough.

"*Dulcha!*" Charles roared, his body covered in blood and burns. His tattoos lit up in a pale gold, active and working.

It just got real.

*****

"Maybe the mark relays location," Andris estimated as he crouched by my head, looking me over.

I blinked blood out of my eye. I'd banged my skull pretty hard on that last lovely little ditty, opening a gash. "What does it matter?" I croaked. "He's here. He knows."

"It matters because he still might not find us." The White Mage flung his cape in a temper as he paced. "If it *is* that mark, which makes the most sense of anything—you took her cell phone?"

"Of course. And we don't have coverage down here, anyway." Andris flexed his gloved hands.

"Right. Well, I can think of nothing else. Which means this will end by killing her. We can then leave some men behind to take him down while we make an escape. We will be safe, this portion of the area will remain undetected, and his forces will be trimmed."

"She has to have more value than a plaything. Stefan wouldn't risk his clan for a pretty human," Andris reasoned.

The White Mage reflected, turning to me. "He's right. What is so exciting about you, girl?"

I laughed sardonically as he stood there, patiently waiting for an answer as though we were chatting over tea. My laugh turned into a wet cough. "I have candy flavored nipples."

Trek scoffed. "Bring in a *Dulcha*. We'll let it feed off her for a few minutes. They tend to have more influence on people like this. Hurry—we need to wrap this up. They're nearly inside."

Intuition said to be ready. Something was about to happen. Some chance would be available for a brief moment, and I'd have to take it then or not at all.

I struggled to sit, puffing through burnt lungs to do it. "That was a helluva punch with magic." I wheezed at a pacing, billowing-caped moron. "You have to show me how you did it one of these days."

He faced me, those pale eyes looking like a blue shirt after it had been bleached. "It takes much more power than a feeble, human *red.*" His smile turned predatory. "But I will give you another demonstration after the *Dulcha* has had its feed."

"Oh good; how exciting."

*****

Stefan stood, bewildered, in the middle of a battle, in the middle of one room of three. He should be standing next to Sasha. He *felt* like he stood next to Sasha. Yet, each of the three rooms was largely bare, holding nothing more than seats and tables.

If he couldn't feel Sasha, he would've thought he'd landed in a trap.

"What next, boss, no one is here!" Charles yelled, twirling between a one-armed man and a *Dulcha* with curved magical horns spraying something similar to acid. The beast took down as many of its own men as his. Maybe more so.

"She should be here," Stefan shouted, stepping toward an oncoming man with a glowing purple sword. Stefan met the man's sword with his own, snapping it in two, then stabbing the body attached to it. "C'mon love, give me a sign."

*****

T he shape blurred as it approached, my brain attempting to blackout in an attempt to escape any more pain. I felt Stefan on top of me, which must mean I was below level. Hence, the cape crusader's assurance he wouldn't find us. So, basically, I had to blow shit up to make some noise.

Luckily, that was one of my specialties. Unluckily, I couldn't reach my damn magic.

A spiked demon came into view. Cross a porcupine with a bull, and you might have it. Worse, glowing red eyes and steam or smoke from its nostrils. The stupid thing was packing power.

My chest warmed as it neared—that special magic elixir these things had, calling to me as usual, but unable to fully affect me with the magic block. It hesitated near my head, turning back to, apparently, its master, the White Mage.

"You make those things, then, huh?" I asked casually, not wanting to hear the answer, but needing to if I ever wanted to beat this clown.

He preened. "Very few in the world can. I've mastered the art."

"Well, whoop-de-doo."

Getting the nod, the spiky creature approached me, glowing eyes staring down. "Join me," it rasped.

"Don't want to," I muttered back, preparing for something awful, though I wasn't sure what.

"What did you say?" the White Mage asked, cocking his head and clutching the corner of his cape.

I didn't get a chance to answer. The block ripped away, the creatures mind trying to attach to mine at the same minute.

This was my chance. I sucked in with all my ability, the sweet rush of pure magic filling me to the brim. The warning spikes prickled my skin just as the demon tried to grasp ahold of my lifeblood.

Usually, I'd settle for red power level, like this cursed monster, just to keep things in check. I couldn't do that now and live. I had to rise above the White Mage in power, because he could beat the hell out of me in actual knowledge.

My palm struck out, the spell to encase the monster in a protective box in my mind. I'd always blown things up when I did this; I figured I'd continue on that road now. A dose of pure black shot out of my palm, eating the dim light as it coalesced around the demon, encasing the monster like it was supposed to.

Except I'd been trying to blow it up.

"Damn it!" I yelled. "*Now* it works? What the hell?"

"Not possible," Trek breathed.

"It is true, then—I hadn't been sure," Andris murmured.

My lower cheeks tingled.

I dove to the side, narrowly missing Andris's grab, willing strength into my shaking body.

Let's try that again.

Using red this time, I did the same spell; only this time, got the desired result. Not only that, but it fed off the magic already there like kerosene.

BOOM!

Small cracks worked through the ceiling. A huge hole developed in the ground.

"It's not possible!" Trek screamed.

"Myth my ass, you egotistical jerk!" I yelled back, rolling against the wall and feeling for earth and fire. Letting loose some previously failed attempts at charms and spells, I blasted red in every direction, feeling out the earth in the land around the basement we occupied. Sure enough, five plants burst through the walls, huge and angry, cement and wood crumbling inward. Vines and giant green leaves, clutching like hands with no fingers, reached.

"What the—" Andris cut off, wide eyed at the monstrous plants.

Every eye in that room, that wasn't occupied with a green thing, turned to me. Yup, the freak had arrived, and even though she didn't have a clue as to what she was doing, she still managed to blow shit up!

"I've got more!" I yelled, summoning back the black. Mayhem was the name of the game until Stefan could get in here and figure a way out.

I threw my palm out, aiming at two men running at me with swords, and tried to fling them backwards. Instead, they gagged, waving their arms in front of their faces like it smelled bad, but kept coming.

"Damn it!" I said again. Why were the spells working now when before they always went haywire?

My butt tingled again. No time to figure it out. I took off running, my eyes searching for a way out.

"Grab her! I need her!" the White Mage screamed.

I dodged a green vine groping into the room and threw

another blast of red toward three vicious looking guys running at me with determination. I hit an ugly couch.

Boom!

The couch shot airborne in the blast, two chairs went sideways. The three men got swept up in a breeze like Mary Poppins. Above them, the ceiling made ominous creaking noises, dirt starting to drizzle.

Another blast rocked the room, only this time, it came from above, where Stefan was. He was trying to get down to us.

"Hurry Stefan," I pleaded, dodging a jet of pure white.

"Get her!" the White Mage screamed again. "We've got to get out of here before this place caves!"

Butt tingle.

I turned to my right just as a monster with bear claws burst through the only exit I could see. It narrowly missed me, and now I had to sprint back into the room, the putrid smell of rot following me. That warning butt pucker had me trying to turn left, but there were more people that way. Huge men with glowing swords had me surrounded, trying to corner the human.

My insides screamed to run just as a glowing white box surrounded me. I swore, tears in my eyes. I didn't know how to get out.

Andris strode toward me as white bands wrapped around my middle.

"She's strong, but she doesn't know her craft!" Trek said, running toward the door. "Keep her confined and bring her with me."

Another explosion sounded above. A massive groan splintered the ceiling. Dirt and debris rained down. Popping and cracks sounded off before a giant chunk of ceiling fell, landing right in front of Trek, making him dive out of the way.

Andris stopped right next to me, staring wide-eyed at the crumbling ceiling.

A man jumped through, narrowly dodging falling objects. He hit the ground and rolled to the side. Blood spilling down his muscle toned arms, strength and brawn tempered with a fluid grace of a swordsmen rose, his eyes like liquid magma as his gaze swept the area. My spine tingled, recognizing that rage and the wrath that would soon follow. Stefan had arrived.

He stepped forward, away from tumbling debris and jumping or falling bodies, meeting two men head on, his tattoos a whitish gold, his sword moving so fast, it looked like a flashlight in a horror movie.

"Bring the girl!" Trek screamed, on his feet and running, *Dulcha* pouring into the room.

Stefan cleaved someone in half, his sword making short work of the second, desperately trying to get to me. Andris squared his body, anticipating the fight with Stefan and unable to turn away from it.

"Don't fight—grab her!" the coward in the white cape screamed as he stood within the doorway, power gathering to him, rolling and boiling.

"Sasha, you have to fight his advance," Stefan said a calm voice crusted with ice. "Suck the power in the room to you. Suck it all in. Close your eyes and draw. I'll balance you through our blood link."

I closed my eyes and did as instructed. My chest got warm immediately, so much magic raging around me.

"It'll kill me to take that much, Stefan!" I cried, fear eating away at me as the building around us started to groan again. The holes from the plants weakened the foundation and the blasts from within and above shaking the place down. Compared to Trek, I was an amateur.

"I'll temper it, love. I'll help." Stefan flung a man out of his way, rending and tearing, meeting a monster with a whirling blade, his eyes now on Andris, the only thing standing in his way.

Besides Trek's magic.

My gaze swept to the caped moron, his face a scary grimace of lethal concentration. His hands braced to the side of him like claws, the magic around his body building. I swung my gaze back to Stefan as he fought his way to me, unconcerned about the magic headed his way, and just trying to get me within his protective embrace.

"Here goes," I whispered.

I closed my eyes again, feeling the elements, feeling the current as it sucked toward Trek like undertow. The feeling slipped through my fingers like water in a stream, tickling my skin. My chest burned now, then my limbs, my power calling to that sweet essence.

I felt the box around me, visibly seeing, in my mind's eye, the weaves and knots that created it. I picked it apart like a sewing stitch, watching it unravel and fall away. I drew in more power, now feeling like insects crawling on my skin. Pure black power level, now, darker than night, sucking in light and turning it into energy. Still the power gathered near Trek.

"Reach for him now," I heard. Stefan's voice seemed so far away. Floating on a distant breeze of magic, eddies and torrents separating the distance between the two of us. Except, I felt him within—loving support, bracing me to the here-and-now. Keeping me firmly rooted.

I did as Stefan said, reaching, feeling the lesser power levels around me, and shooing them away like fruit flies. I found that boiling collection of magic an instant before it released, and put up a shield.

His power blasted into mine, two solid things colliding like rams in a mating dance. The sound thundered, shaking the building, knocking everyone off their feet. Except for me and Trek.

His eyes burned into mine, not working the elements, just sucking them in and throwing them at me. Dumb move, because that was about all I could do, too. I dug in my feet magically and pushed, as hard as I could, the swirling magic of his attack spell inching back toward him.

"Suck it in, Sasha! Consume it. This place is collapsing."

I heard distant metal clanging. The building roaring. Voices shouting and screaming. Still, I stared at those pale blue eyes, the sky seen through an overexposed picture. I could win this war of might, but it would take too long. Plus, if he grew some brains and stopped thinking with his testosterone, he'd realize all he had to do was switch it up a bit and I'd be lost.

Closing my eyes, hoping this wasn't the end, I did as Stefan said. I opened myself up, let go of the corporal world around me, and sucked with one painful, scorching draw.

CHAPTER TEN

WHY THE HELL WAS I ALWAYS COMING TO OUT OF A DEEP sleep? Was that my default in dangerous situations—passing out?

"What was that, love?"

Stefan sat at the edge of my bed, holding my hand. Bruises and gashes marred his handsome face, and cuts and scrapes gouged his body; but he was alive. I was alive.

"I *am* alive, right?" I clarified.

He smiled. "Yes, you saved the day."

I chuckled then winced. My whole body felt unnaturally sensitive. "What happened after I took in the magic?"

"You passed out." Charles sat in the corner, knitting needles thrashing out the finishing touches of the hideous scarf he was making me.

"What happened to you?" I asked in a voice tinged with fear.

Half of Charles's body had splatters of burn marks, like he'd dropped something heavy in liquid magma and it splashed out onto his skin. "I had to cut through that fucking—"

"Language," Stefan warned.

Charles sighed, but continued. "I had to cut through that *freaking* spell that Darla never taught us about. Andris has the same power level as me. It hurt. A lot."

"He exacted his own penance for your capture," Stefan said mildly.

"Thanks, Boss," Charles muttered.

Something passed between them, but since I wouldn't be able to decipher it anyway, and Charles wouldn't fill me in until Stefan left, I skipped ahead. "How am I alive after sucking in that much magic? I feel like Charles looks, only on the inside."

Charles snorted.

Stefan brushed hair off of my face, and then laid his palm flat to my cheek. "I balanced it. Tempered it, you might say. Everyone has a unique strength with magic. Mine has always been orchestrating the flow, whether in myself or others. With enemies, it allows me to direct it in hard to work places in the body, lessening their ability. In you, I was able to fill up every square inch of your beautiful body, balancing the abundance. It was close, I'm not going to lie to you—I took a great risk that I'm not proud of—but I could see no other way."

I couldn't help but stare. "I did not know any of that was even possible."

"There is a lot you don't know. Which is why I have requested a master trainer. With your power level, they cannot say no."

I groaned, letting my head fall back. "I need a break from magic. My body hurts. Again."

Stefan smiled, a sight that had my heart pattering and my groin tightening. "Of course."

"So, aside from your heroics with magic usage, how did we get out of that building?" I pushed.

Stefan bent to my lips and carefully kissed me. He backed off and stood. "I'll let Charles explain. I need to see to the wounded. I'll check in later." He winked, and then was off.

When it was just Charles and me, I said, "Well?"

"I hope you don't plan to be grouchy. I've had a bad couple of days and I'm not in the mood for your sass."

"My days haven't been any better."

"Yes, but I am the man, and men suffer more thoroughly than women. Everyone knows this."

"So, I just ask you if that's true, right?"

"Exactly. We know better, and we suffer more. Facts."

"That scarf is ugly."

"We also have better taste."

I couldn't help a laugh. "Please tell me?"

Click, click, click.

He sighed, loving to make me wait. "Well, first you stole everyone's magic in the whole room. That idiot in the cape stared at you like a spoiled little brat who had his candy stolen. He ran, of course. Cowardly little bitch. You collapsed, as you do; so, the Boss lost his mind, as he does. He sliced and gouged Andris, nearly had him beat, before the building started to collapse. You almost got smooshed, which stopped the Boss's fight right quick. Andris let the Boss have you as he ran after the man in the costume."

"The man in the costume?"

"The caped moron—keep up. Right, so now the Boss has his prize. His men—us—have a victory nearly at hand, and the danged ceiling comes tumbling down. It turned out to be a narrow miss. With just a trickle of magic, and whatever he must have siphoned off you in your link, the boss had to blast his way out of a wall, hand you off to me, and get all his people out of there. He very nearly went down with the ship."

"Stefan almost died?" I whispered, fear and sorrow at the possibility choking me.

"That's his duty—make sure his people are safe. He wouldn't be a leader so young if he couldn't see to it."

I closed my eyes, my body shaking.

Click, click, click.

"Good news is, we destroyed their hideout. The building had a tunnel leading from their territory to ours. We couldn't detect them crossing through because our spells are all above ground, and they were below it. Obviously. Hence the word 'tunnel.' So, we should be back to right where that's concerned. Plus, you shook up Trek—he thought he held the most power in this corner of the world. Now there's you. If we can get you trained, we can have some *real* battles! Let you deal with him so the rest of us can beat the piss out of the Eastern Territory!"

The glee in Charles' voice was unmistakable.

"You nearly died, you're burnt to hell, but you're *excited* about more battles to come. What the hell is wrong with you?"

"In a nutshell? I still have to be your bodyguard. Although, you are entertaining, I'll say that much. If your moods weren't so bad, it might be a fun gig."

"If *my* moods weren't so bad? You have way worse PMS than I do!"

Charles raised his chin with an important air about him. "I am a man—I am not moody, I am stressed because I am important."

I shook my head with a smile. "Idiot."

*****

I t took me two days to get on my feet. Stefan told me he wouldn't have sex with me because he worried about my wellbeing; but when I took blood from him, then climbed in his lap, the fight went out of him.

We ate breakfast and dinner together, and slept in the same bed—a practice he wanted to continue forever. I wasn't so sure. What would happen when he had to take a mate? Three people in a bed were too many for my taste. Plus, I wouldn't be able to share him. I didn't want another woman so much as looking at him for too long. It made our future extremely uncertain.

Add to that a bigwig coming to this clan specifically to evaluate my strange and usually not working brand of magic and...I needed a fast ride. I hadn't made Charles scream yet, but I wanted to give it another try.

"Hurry up!" Charles yelled. He'd been waylaid with me, not admitting he needed time to heal. Thankfully, he didn't have to. He was still my bodyguard, so he got to rest while I did. So, now that we took the opportunity to go for a drive, in which I would absolutely speed, he was antsy.

"Jesus, slow your roll. I had to put on my shoe—" I cut off.

Sitting in the driver's seat of my car, wearing a black and gold bowtie, was a 'me' sized teddy bear.

"What the hell is that?" Charles asked, staring.

I smiled, my heart filling with love. I felt an answering warmth through our shared link. "Stefan is fulfilling his duty."

The drive was fantastic, flying over hills and speeding around turns. I felt as light as air. Charles swore three times. And all the while, the teddy bear was in the back, bouncing around like it was in a jumpy-house, grinning happily—a symbol of the love Stefan and I shared.

∽

Sign up to be the FIRST to know when the next book goes live. Plus get newsletter only bonus content for FREE. Click here to sign up.

ON A RAZOR'S EDGE (BOOK 3)

Sasha's journey continues in:

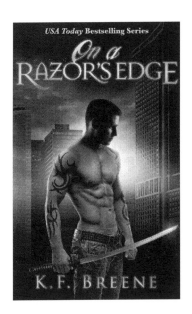

Chapter 1

A smile flashed across Stefan's breathtakingly handsome face in the failing evening light. "You are so hell bent on not blasting me, you aren't working the blade. Try again."

I bounced from foot to foot like a football player waiting for *hike*. Stefan stood in front of me, large sword held lightly, waiting for me to strike. I feinted left and dove right, slashing with my very sharp dagger. The blade hacked down toward his forearm, making me squint in fear that I would hit him, until he easily shifted at the last second. The blade swept by toward the ground.

Stefan's laughter echoed off the trees as he wrapped his big tattooed arms around my middle to keep me from landing on my head.

This was his special tutoring. Getting up before nightfall, sneaking out to the wooded area behind his mansion, hanging out in a bunch of trees, and laughing at me as he tried to teach me to use my dagger. I failed to see the humor.

"That was good," Stefan commended. "I like the feint. Believable."

I sighed with the feel of him. His strength. His *power*. The man was made well. Very well.

"Hmmm, chocolate chip cookies. I would love to eat you right now." His lips trailed up my neck as tingles worked between my thighs. I melted into his arms as he sucked the hot skin on my neck. "But we need to get you using that dagger, so I'll wait."

"We have plenty of time for training," I breathed.

Ignoring my roaming hands, he propped me up, held me away from him for a moment so my Gumby legs could straighten out, then stepped away with a mouth-watering smile.

I tried to force my frazzled brain back to the situation. "Except, I missed with that feint. Which, don't get me wrong, is a good thing, since if I'd hit you you'd be missing an arm, but still. I can't be *that* good. My comic timing, however, seems to be perfect..."

"Sorry, lovely, I can't help it. Your face goes through all these expressions. Determination first, pa-zazz with the feint, fear when you think you'll get me, and finally relief right before you land on your face. It's comical. You have no poker face."

"You've known how to play poker for, literally, forty-eight hours. How would you know about poker face? And what is a *pa-zazz* face?"

Stefan laughed again. "I've been beating you at poker for, *literally,* the last twenty-four hours," he mocked. "I like that we upped the stakes. The sexual benefits make it much more fun."

Being without much money of my own my whole life, I'd always played poker with friends for tokens. Stefan didn't really get the point of the card game using peanuts, though, so I switched it to strip poker. That got his attention. Then he got the idea to bet sexual favors.

He got really good shortly thereafter. I found myself in some pretty kinky poses with other...paraphernalia that turned out to be quite a lot of fun—for special occasions.

"Beginner's luck," I commented sourly. "And that was only one game."

"Several hands in one game, yes. With lots of breaks for touching. I'm one-for-two. After the end of tonight, I'll be two-for-three. And pleasured often."

"Okay, Texas Hold 'Em, focus for one second. Why can't I make you bleed?" I got back in my ready stance: hands out, knees slightly bent, balls of my feet.

"I'm the best."

"And modest to boot."

He shrugged, waiting patiently for me to try and kill him.

I lunged without warning, jabbing for his heart. He

stepped right lazily, flicking my dagger away with his sword, the tattoos on his arms glowing gently.

"You aren't connecting with your magic. That's the problem." He focused on my red blade. "You need to use all your power, not just your safety zone."

"I don't want to blow you up, Stefan," I answered seriously, jogging to a stop three paces beyond him. "Red at least is manageable if something goes wrong. If I use black, who knows, you know?"

His smile dwindled. His black eyes regarded me softly. "We have help coming. They'll know how to train you. They'll know what to do."

What he was too kind to say was, "They'll know why your magic doesn't work like everyone else's." His hope, and mine, was that they could explain why I was different.

All I wanted was to fit in. But Fate continually wanted me the butt of every joke. We were at war, Fate and me. And guess what, Fate was winning. And an asshole.

"Okay, more power, coming up." I breathed deeply, opening to the world around me.

Instantly a gush of power flooded my body, raging and flowing, pushing in to fill up every inch. I sent Stefan a panicked look.

Immediately he was there, through the link between us, using his special ability to smooth it all out. Temper it. Balance it.

Elation tingled as the magic swirled and pooled, stretching my skin, making me high. When he was within me, balancing it all out, *God* I felt good. Masterful. Freaking fantastic!

"Hee yaw, waaka waaka." I bounced like a boxer and shook out my limbs. "Feeling good. Feeling really good."

Stefan nodded slowly, his beautiful onyx eyes twinkling. "It gives the feeling of ecstasy if it's balanced right. The blood link—the tie to me—boosts it tenfold, though. It never felt as good to hold max capacity before we developed the blood link."

His love for me, pulsing through the link, warmed my insides. I smiled like a fool before reality came crashing down. "It seems like it's getting worse, though. I give a soft tug on the elements and I get a flood, whereas before, I had to actively pull before the avalanche came down."

All remnants of a smile vanished. "Starting after puberty, we get stronger the more we work with the elements. It's a steady climb until we reach maximum potential, which happens in everyone at different times. Maybe it's similar with you."

"The more I work with the elements, the more open I am to receive them?" I frowned at him. It kind of made sense. "Except I'm already at full power."

"You've had a rough control over your magic for years without knowing it. You've had more than enough time to reach max potential, but maybe now, being more open with the elements, it'll come easier."

"But why is it such a struggle to contain it all?" I asked sullenly, punctuating the question by stabbing the air.

Stefan minutely shook his head as he studied my mood. "But you do have a lot of power, and with me to balance it out within you, you *are* learning control. With some better instruction, and your intuition, you'll be dynamite."

I couldn't help but chuckle. "Dyn-o-mite."

I got a quirked head in response.

"Never mind. There's no use in us trying to figure this out. Let's just hope the guy that's coming has a clue."

Stefan dropped his sword and stepped forward so fast I got a nervous flutter he was attacking me. Only, I was still too slow to jab him. He flicked away my dagger and laid a palm on my cheek. "He will. We'll figure this out, you and me. You aren't in this alone. I've pledged my life to you—I'm in this with you, whatever it turns out to be."

My eyes misted over with the sentiment. His soft lips brushed mine, the kiss slow and ardent. Expressing his love. Speeding up my heart.

I slid my hand down his defined chest and let it rest on his bumpy abs. "I can't figure out control over my magic, but I can figure out how to poke things, so I guess I'll get good at that until these mysterious helpers roll through."

He gave me one last soft kiss before backing up. His lips curled into a smile. "That's my girl. Learn to kill monsters while you're waiting for the next great thing."

"The next big thing. Is here. That's an ad. I swear, you and Charles are researching my quirks in the wrong ways. My crazy is not a human problem—it's specific to me."

"It's a good place to start. And the next big thing has been here. Or didn't you remember getting pounded by it when you woke up?"

I rolled my eyes. "No need to get crude—you're a man, I hear you roar. Now, prepare to die."

I lunged at him, magic racing through my limbs, buzzing through my midsection. He rolled away from my blade, barely missed. His glowing sword came up as my dagger sped toward his midsection, blocking at the last moment. On the move again.

"As—" He feinted, making me pivot at the last second, falling behind.

"You—" His sword rushed toward me, causing me to take two fast steps left and smash my dagger against his steel. He was already moving again.

"Wish!" The very tip of his blade flicked at my ribcage, opening a little tear in my shirt.

I flinched back, panting. Hands on knees, I caught my

breath while huffing out a laugh. "Charles had you watch some of the romantic comedies, huh?"

"A few."

"Had a good laugh at the men in them, I'd bet."

"Soft men paired with soft women. That fits."

I straightened up, confronted by his lighthearted smile. "And I am...?"

"Irresistible. Beautiful. *Mine*."

Warm fuzzies permeated my chest. Until he finished with, "Also from a race with terrible romance movies."

His laughter echoed once again. I figured it was a great time to try and jab him unexpectedly.

~~~~~~~

Buy it now: On a Razor's Edge

ABOUT THE AUTHOR

K.F. Breene is a USA TODAY BESTSELLING author of the Darkness Series and Warrior Chronicles. She lives in wine country where over every rolling hill, or behind every cow, an evil sorcerer might be plotting his next villainous deed while holding a bottle of wine and brick of cheese. Her husband thinks she's cracked for wandering around, muttering about magic and swords. Her kids are on board with her fantastical imagination, except when the description of the monsters becomes too real.

She'll wait until they're older to tell them that monsters are real, and so is the magic to fight them. She wants them to sleep through the night, after all...

Join the reader group to chat with her personally: https://goo.gl/KAgoNr

Want to stay in the loop?
Sign up to be the FIRST to learn about new releases. Plus get

newsletter only bonus content for FREE. Click here to sign up.

Contact info:
kfbreene.com/
kfbreene@gmail.com

OTHER TITLES BY K.F. BREENE

Jonas

Charles

Jameson

Want to stay in the loop?

Sign up to be the FIRST to learn about new releases. Plus get newsletter only bonus content for FREE. Click here to sign up.

68041783R00098

Made in the USA
Columbia, SC
03 August 2019

Made in the USA
Middletown, DE
18 July 2020

D1525346

RETURN OF
THE LORD

*Narrative Reflections on the
Apostles' Final Moments*

RETURN OF THE LORD

Narrative Reflections on the Apostles' Final Moments

Michael Creavey

For my brother Joe and all the seminarians discerning Jesus Christ's call to the priesthood throughout the world: Thank you for believing in this project and insisting that I publish it!

CONTENTS

AUTHOR'S NOTE

This project was conceived, sustained, and completed in an atmosphere of prayer. I wrote most of these reflections longhand on yellow legal pads at all hours of the day and night in the presence of Our Lord, and at first it was not a conscious attempt to "create" anything, really. But writing a book turns out to be a rather unpredictable experience! Though this volume is relatively brief, it took me well over four years to complete it once the thought first occurred to me.

It all began with a very simple image that emerged in prayer when we were living in State College, Pennsylvania. My wife Kristine and I had not been married for long and I was facing a challenging teaching semester. I was feeling frustrated by some work-related drama that had recently cropped up and I had not been finding much consolation in prayer. It seemed like no matter what I tried, I was unable to focus, and my prayer was characterized almost entirely by worry and distraction.

One day, I thought I'd give it another try by heading to a nearby chapel and just sitting there for an hour or so. I didn't bring a Bible, a notebook, or

anything else with me this time. I merely sat there allowing myself to be enveloped by the silence of the empty sanctuary while I stared at the tabernacle. After a while, something unexpected started to happen. I began to think about Jesus' apostles. This alone wasn't particularly unusual because these men and their unique role in the life and ministry of Jesus is a meditation that ceaselessly intrigues me. What was different this time was the intensity and clarity of what I saw. It was as though I was standing in their midst as they gathered together in fellowship, but they couldn't see me. I looked at them intently and I paid attention to every detail: their clothes, eye colors, skin tones, the way they spoke and the way they laughed. I felt gradually overwhelmed by the vividly realistic setting to which my heart and mind were leading me, and I grew utterly fascinated with all of them.

The apostles were not remarkable by any of the standards by which we typically measure how much a person merits our serious attention. They were fishermen, carpenters, even tax collectors. They were not religious scholars (except Paul, but more on him later), priests, rabbis, or "experts" in the eyes of 1st century Jews. And yet, the Lord chose them. As he himself says in John 15:16, "It was not you who chose me, but I who chose you and appointed you to go and bear fruit that will remain, so that whatever you ask the Father in my name he may give you." They were flawed to a man. They could be strong and courageous, but more often

than not they were as quickly beset by fear, confusion, and foolishness due to the fog brought about by sin as any of us are today. *How unimpressive and "ordinary" you all were!* I almost laughed to myself while in their midst.

And then it happened. I imagined one of them in particular, caught in the throes of his astonishing martyrdom (I won't spoil your reading by telling you who just yet!) He was deeply afflicted, strongly tempted by fear and the promise of a reprieve if only he would recant his faith and reject the Lord. But something was different now. He was not the man he had been when he was young - he was so much more. He was wrapped up in mystery, held up by an invisible power that no one around him during this ghastly episode would allow themselves to see. He was, in a word, resolute. Out of nowhere, I suddenly saw the Risen Jesus approaching his dying friend, his face radiating purest joy as he reached out to draw the faithful one to himself forever.

Just as swiftly as this meditation had begun, it faded away and I was alone once more in the chapel. I was completely at peace, filled with wonder and awe, entirely captivated by the contrast between who this sinful man had been and who he had become. *What could possibly produce that kind of transformation?* I thought. *How could anyone change that much?* Because he did change. There is no question about it. It is a matter of historical fact. And that change did not only affect him. It literally affected the entire world.

I rushed home, grabbed a pen and paper and began my first draft of the book you now hold, never imagining that this one narrative reconstruction would grow into meditations on all of them in their final moments. But if you don't yet know that that is precisely God's style, I can't wait for you to get to know him more!

Once I had the idea for this book crystalizing in my mind, the challenge came of attempting to situate these reflections in as historically accurate a way as possible. This was more challenging for some of Jesus' friends than others. While we of course learn about the fates of two apostles in the pages of Scripture (Judas, Jesus' betrayer and James, son of Zebedee who was executed by Herod in Acts 12) we learn little or nothing at all about the others' earthly ends there. So what happened to them? You may be surprised to learn that ancient traditions regarding each apostle's life, ministry, and death following the Resurrection have been passed down for centuries. While some of these traditions are more historically verifiable than others, the history major in me was keenly interested in rooting each meditation in firm, reliable tradition.

One of the difficulties that arose is that there are oftentimes different, even conflicting details scattered throughout these apostolic traditions. When you start digging as I did, you'll quickly discover that some traditions claim this apostle was crucified while others claim he was drowned, beaten or stoned to death, or thrown down from a high

place. Apostle X is reputed to have been killed in Egypt, India, Persia, and Jerusalem. Well… Which is it?!

Early on in the project, I decided that I would not let myself get too fixated on the exact circumstances, but rather I would try in such disputed cases to lean on the most agreed upon details and, when needed, craft a composite that seemed to me a faithful presentation of the remarkably deep faith each one of these men possessed. Furthermore, the sequence in which I present their stories generally reflects the chronological order in which the apostles died, not necessarily the order in which I wrote the reflections. Through it all, the goal was simple. I wanted to read compelling narrative reconstructions of the final moments of these inspiring men. I couldn't really find anything like that out there, so I thought *I'd* write them!

Just to whet your appetite a bit with a few intriguing details I learned along the way, I would first mention the discovery that "Bartholomew" literally means "son of Talmai". Keep an eye out for that as you read because in the spirit of inspired creative license, I addressed it. I kept finding myself wondering *Who was Talmai? Does that really matter? What was his relationship like with Bartholomew?* I only mention this in passing and if you blink, you'll miss it, but it was interesting to ponder nonetheless. And if I'm completely off base, Nathanael please forgive me!

Another intriguing question that arose during my research was that of Jesus' "brothers", or better translated "cousins" or "kin". Ancient Hebrew did not have a proper word for the latter, and the extended family culture of the Israelites often made it a moot point (ex. Abraham calls Lot his "brother" in Genesis 14 even though Lot is his nephew). That being said, there are several different traditions about Our Lord's family relations with certain apostles and I drew from several of those to hopefully enhance some of the drama in a way you have not seen before.

As a Catholic, I wanted to ensure that this book wasn't something only Catholics would find helpful and inspiring. I firmly hope, pray, and believe that any Christian reader will be able to find at least something in this text that strengthens his or her faith. That being said, there are a few little hints peppered throughout the book that connect certain apostles with patronages or images for which they have become known through the centuries in Catholic devotional life. Most of these references are subtle, but I hope you'll enjoy them when you see them - I know I do! None of them were really planned ahead of time and I was delighted when they worked their way into the text.

Another thing I want to mention is that God loves to change people's names! Oftentimes in the Bible, a new calling brings with it a new name (ex. Jacob becomes Israel, Simon becomes Peter, etc.) There is a brief, albeit ambiguous, mention in the

writings of the Church Father Clement of Alexandria (AD 150-215) that Matthias, successor to Judas, was in fact one in the same as a figure we meet briefly in Luke's Gospel during Jesus' ministry. Suffice it to say that if this is true, Matthias, like the others, began on a much different path than the one to which Our Lord called him. That's why I thought I'd try this obscure little tradition on for size for this project.

Finally, I would like to mention the prologue and epilogue in passing (please don't cheat by reading ahead!) The decision to add these came last, and I will merely say that a beautifully consoling thought kept arising throughout the project that I think prompted the addition. Jesus Christ is God, but so too is he fully man. The unfathomable wonder and beauty of his human relationships is a source of lifelong meditation and joy, for he calls you and me to have our own unique, unrepeatable relationships with him. And that glorious yet simple reality of the Son of God entering into human relationship began and was nourished for nearly thirty years in the humble home of the Holy Family. Trust me, meditating on that household is an inexhaustible treasure in the spiritual life.

This manuscript was somehow both tremendously easy to write, and tremendously difficult. It was a joyful process, and an emotionally draining one. If you're anything like me, some portions of this book will bring a smile to your face while others will be very challenging to get through.

The bottom line is, these men willingly faced the most gruesome sufferings and death rather than abandon Jesus Christ. Not one of them seems to have been suited for such trials on the basis of his own personality, strength, or willpower. The Holy Spirit of God, living in each one of them, enabled them to do so much more than just suffer and die for some cause. They suffered Christ's own suffering, and they died his own death. In my view this radical, transformative participation in Christ's own life is the single most important takeaway for your own meditation and prayer. I pray that our Lord richly blesses all those who read this work, and I hope above all that in reading it, you will be as inspired to grow in relationship with Him as I was in writing it.

Michael Creavey
June 29, 2020
Feast of Saints Peter and Paul

Translation Note: Any portions of this text that quote Sacred Scripture directly or that have a clear biblical reference point are drawing from either the New American Bible, Revised Edition or the Revised Standard Version, Catholic Edition translations.

PROLOGUE

The man kept moving around the enormous, pitch-black cell like he always did. He needed to check on a few more prisoners. There were new ones brought here every day, and he could not help but care for them. A reassuring word, a loving embrace from his sturdy arms seemed to bring great comfort to them all. They trusted him and when he told them help was on the way and would soon arrive, they believed him.

He looked around, squinting in the blackness. It was truly miserable here. The air was dry and hot and dusty. The ground was hard and sharp with jagged rocks strewn about. He could never see clearly enough to make out the features of any fellow prisoners when he was with them for that place had never known the light.

The only things he could see clearly were the guards. They were huge, ominous, beastly creatures. They prowled and growled and reveled in their malice. Cruel without a trace of pity, they were harder than the stone from which the colossal cell had been hewn. And yet, even the constant pursuit of their devious desires could bring them no joy. They always did what they wanted to do, and they

hated every minute of it. If they had ever known love or joy or bliss, it had been very long ago indeed.

The man soon came upon a new prisoner, huddled in a rock-ribbed corner and weeping fearfully. The poor soul was startled by the sudden attention.

"Friend," said the man, "are you alright?"

"Where am I?" asked the other with a tremble.

"The Prison," replied the man.

He could see only the faintest outline of the new cellmate, but it was obvious that he was trying to make out his surroundings to no avail.

"What's your name?" asked the man.

The new prisoner had to think for a few seconds, but then he replied, "Dismas... What's yours?"

"My name is Joseph, Dismas, and I am very pleased to meet you." Quiet for a moment, Joseph went on, "What's the last thing you remember?"

Dismas struggled to collect his thoughts as calmly as possible, though the ambiance of this frightful setting complicated things. The presence of this compassionate cellmate helped put him at ease. His thoughts became clearer and began to come into focus.

"I... I was on a hill outside the city," he muttered slowly, retracing the steps of his journey to this place in his mind.

"What city?" asked Joseph.

"Jerusalem--" Dismas hushed abruptly as a monstrous guard lumbered past them, glancing their way with an ancient scowl and snarl.

"Can you remember what happened next?" asked Joseph, encouraging him to continue. "Try, my friend, please try."

"There were two others with me," he strained to help the image in his mind focus once more. "I'm remembering now! Yes! It's coming back to me! One of them was my friend--"

The last word fell from his lips like an anchor. It brought him to a complete stop and his dismay at this recollection was palpable. Several silent moments passed between them.

"Your friend, you say?" Joseph prodded gently.

"He *was* my friend... and we were terrible men. We robbed. We plundered. We lied and cheated and ruined lives..." he trailed off and began to sob.

Joseph put his arm around the forlorn prisoner's shoulders and patted his back firmly. *My father used to do that*, Dismas thought. He mused in passing that his new friend must have been a stone worker or perhaps a carpenter. He seemed to possess both a remarkable strength and an unusual gentleness all at once. The new prisoner was deeply consoled by his presence.

"Who was the other?" Joseph asked.

"The other?" Dismas replied before coming once more to a degree of lucidity in the gloomy cell. "Yes! Him! Oh, I can hardly describe him, sir! Like us, he was condemned to die. But I couldn't understand

why. The journey from the praetorium to the hill outside the city was torture, yet he refused to curse his accusers. He didn't resist any of the torment or ridicule from the soldiers or the crowd. He even *prayed* for them! Can you believe that? He prayed for them! It was almost as if--"

"As if he was *meant* to suffer and to die?" asked Joseph with a mysterious, solemn tone.

"Yes... yes that's exactly what I was about to say! How did you--"

"Please," insisted Joseph, "tell me what happened next."

"We, the three of us, were crucified on that hill. It was... I cannot even describe the agony. All I can tell you for certain is that I regretted everything the moment the hammer began to do its work. I regretted my whole life - my wicked sins, the way I treated so many people. All the while, I couldn't stop looking at that other crucified man between the two of us. They said his name was Jesus, from Nazareth in Galilee. They treated him so much more brutally than us, I don't understand it."

Dismas could have sworn he heard Joseph quietly gasp back tears in the shadows, but he could not tell for sure. He continued the account.

"I knew I was not going to live much longer. None of us would. I had this urge welling up in me to say something to that poor man. I felt that if I could just confess my wickedness to him, somehow he could make it right. I don't know. I'm not sure you could understand."

Joseph's grin went unseen, but it was quite real and sincere.

"Oh, I understand far better than you might think," he said. "What did you say to him, then?"

"It was so hard to speak at all, but somehow I managed. I looked into his eyes, eyes like the light of the sun, and I simply said, 'Lord! Remember me when you come into your kingdom!'"

"What did he say back? Did he reply?" implored Joseph in a new tone that was so filled with eagerness that it startled the new prisoner.

"He said, 'Amen, I say to you, on this day you will be with me in paradise.'"

Joseph clasped his calloused hands together and began to do the strangest thing, at least in that dreadful place. He laughed. He laughed with such a boisterous and triumphant vigor the prison's walls seemed to shake. It was a laugh unlike anyone had ever heard, the laugh of a man who knew Good News that no one else did and that he could not wait to share.

"What is it? Why do you laugh, sir?" a confused Dismas inquired.

At that moment, he realized that it had not been his imagination. The walls *were* shaking, and more violently with each passing second. Guards snorted and growled in agitation. Terrified prisoners throughout the cavernous cell began to cry out and run, stumbling and tripping over one another and the jagged rocks. Through it all his new friend continued to laugh, through gradually he eased into

an inexplicable calm. He turned once more to Dismas and placed his hands on his shoulders.

"My friend, are you ready to leave this place?"

Before the other could answer there came an ear-splitting crash at the huge iron cell door not far from where they stood. Dismas flinched and cried out in shock. Joseph did not. Chaos ensued as guards fumbled around in a state of panic. Suddenly the door burst open into the cell and crashed mightily down upon several howling guards. Blinding light poured in from the outside. The other guards fled in terror for the shadows like insects beneath a rock lifted up under the midday sun.

Dismas had fallen to the dusty floor, but he soon felt two strong yet gentle hands helping him up. It was his new friend, whom he could now see clearly in the glorious light pouring into the cell. Joseph was of medium height, robust with leathered skin clearly worn by many years of intense labor. Graying hair, yet somehow youthful, he looked deeply into Dismas' eyes and spoke once more.

"I said, are you ready to leave this place? Forever?"

"Yes!" replied the new prisoner. "Yes, I am!"

"Good. Because he's here," Joseph said gesturing toward the frame of the obliterated cell door.

Dismas now saw in bewilderment that the light was emanating from a person in the doorway, brighter than all the stars in the night sky. He squinted until his eyes adjusted enough to make out

who it was. It was *him* - the Innocent One from Golgotha. He was alive again! How could he be alive again? Prisoners streamed toward the door in droves and the Risen One ushered them through like a shepherd guiding his flock through a gate. Dismas followed them joyfully and never looked back.

After some time had passed, there remained but one soul in that dismal place. Joseph had sought out everyone he could find and had led them one by one to the door. Now there was no one left - he had made sure of that. Just then he heard a voice behind him. He knew it so well, the voice he had first heard as the tiny cry of a newborn in a cave, and it brought tears to his eyes to hear it now.

"Abba," the voice said as a hand with a large wound through which the saving light could be seen reached out to him. "Come home."

CHAPTER ONE

James the Greater

Sweat dripped from James' brow to the dusty ground on which he knelt. Though he trembled somewhat under the blistering Jerusalem sun, he was not filled with terror. The rage of the crowd demanding that his blood be spilt was thick in the air. The executioner stood poised at James' right side, sharpened blade in hand and awaiting his commander's signal to strike the fatal blow.

James' eyes scanned the crowd one last time as he breathed deliberately and deeply. He closed his eyes. To his surprise he sensed a strange rush, like a blustering wind stirring him to the core. The light grew dim and the noise of the frenzied mob dissipated until all he could hear was the distant chirping of crickets in the dead of night. Startled, James looked around in hurried fashion. He was utterly disoriented, yet it took only moments for him to realize where he was.

Gethsemane, the garden at the foot of the Mount of Olives. He was back in Gethsemane on that fateful night. Of all the places his mind could have taken him at this critical hour! To be here once

more was a tortuous thing indeed. It put a pit in his stomach, for he had run through the events of that night so many times he had lost count. James saw it all now, right before his eyes, every detail precisely as he remembered it. Every stone, every star in the sky, every intricate scent of the olive trees and the garden from which they sprung came to him once more.

As he took in the familiar scene he saw the tree off to his right, thick and ancient, olives exploding from its branches as spring was once more upon them. At the base of the tree sat three men, propped against the massive trunk and rapt in a deep slumber. Peter sat in the middle, peacefully breathing like a child gently napping without a care in the world. To his right was John, so young and energetic. To see John asleep had always seemed strange, for no one was more alert and alive. Last of all sat James himself.

He stared for some time at his younger self. He still could not believe he had been here that night, sleeping as the Lord suffered so deeply. Recalling this, James turned and gazed into the fog. He knew where to look. Sure enough, there he was. The Lord knelt about a stone's throw away and he trembled as though some unseen terror sat upon his shoulders. He prayed without ceasing, bent down under the phantom weight.

"Father!" James overheard him exclaim. "Let this chalice pass from me!"

In his slumber, James had not heard the Lord's words that night. He inched closer in order to hear more clearly.

"But... not my will... Thy will be done!"

James stared at the Lord. Here and now, he could not take his eyes off him. His face was spotted with blood! How could he have failed to notice that before? It pierced his heart to realize that his shame could deepen still more despite the glorious years which had followed this night, the darkest of nights.

James was still pouring over all this when the crowd began to emerge from the shadows, men with torches and clubs, swords and shackles approaching like an impending storm. The Lord arose, firm and resolute as any man could be. But he was no ordinary man. His composure was nothing short of divine.

Next came Judas who stepped forward and kissed the Lord on the cheek, hailing him as "rabbi." *Oh Judas,* James lamented, *how we all sorrowed for you! How we sorrow still!* No sooner had this notion entered his mind than James watched helplessly as the mob violently seized the Lord. Like a ghost, a vaporous memory, James saw the scene unfold but was helpless to intervene.

"No! Let him go!" He shouted in vain. "I'm the one you want! Take me instead!"

But even as he cried out so sincerely the terrible truth of the memory did not change. James watched himself standing not twenty feet from the Lord as the armed men pummeled him and chained his

wrists and ankles. His younger self looked petrified, crippled by fear like he had never known before. And then came the dreadful moment that he had never been able to forget.

The younger James turned, and he ran away. He fled the scene as fast as his legs would carry him and he never looked back. That was what had happened that night. James had abandoned the one he said he loved more than anything, even more than his own life. He betrayed his Lord. He betrayed his friend. *Who am I to condemn Judas? Did not I likewise hand the Lord over to death?* James felt utterly hollow, empty, devoid of anything but disgust and shame. A solitary tear fell from his shuttered eyes and mingled with the dust on which he knelt. Suddenly he sensed light all around him. It was hot. The cool night air vanished as quickly as it had appeared, and the distinct aromas of the garden slipped away, replaced by the arid breeze and the smell of the angry crowd.

James opened his eyes. Bloodthirsty cries for the executioner to get on with it rose up like a tidal wave of fury and hatred. Still shaken by the vision and the dark memories, James almost failed to notice the man who approached and knelt directly before him. Nobody else seemed to notice him either. Perhaps no one cared. James looked up, his eyes still adjusting to the blinding sunlight. He gasped. The Lord knelt before him. James could only stare at him in awe and a flurry of emotions. As their eyes met, he simply smiled at James.

That smile washed over James in an instant, like a gentle wave removing every mark from a scarred shore. The Lord knew everything. He knew James straight through, scars and all. And yet nothing, not even the betrayal of that night in the garden would keep him from his beloved friend. James knew the sword was descending, but he no longer feared anything. He would never run away again, and he knew it now in his heart of hearts.

Those in the crowd saw only a dying man who said something so quietly it was almost inaudible.

He said, "Thank you, Lord."

The sword fell, and all was silent.

CHAPTER TWO

Philip

The news traveled swiftly in Hierapolis that morning. It was cool throughout the city – cold even. Clouds swept across the pale blue sky as though they had somewhere to be, and in the shadows they cast below crowds gathered to see the man they had been hearing about for some time.

He was not much to look at. Somewhat haggard, graying curly hair and a grizzled beard, the man looked like the kind of nondescript person one might pass in the marketplace every day and never notice. There was one thing about him though that caused some in the crowd to pause for a moment, fixed in a mysterious sense of curiosity - his eyes. If asked to describe them, anyone in the crowd could have detailed their size, color, shape and the like. Yet what many sensed but could not have put into words was that they were eyes that had beheld a deep wonder. They were the eyes of a man who had seen many things he could not explain but that he would nevertheless proclaim to the ends of the earth. These eyes had witnessed anguish and dashed hopes. But so too had they seen the utterly joyful, triumphant, and magnificent. They were

redeemed eyes, and they belonged to Philip, the apostle of Jesus of Nazareth.

For his part, Philip seemed strangely at peace on this morning of gloom. Considering the scene just a few paces before him, this struck those in the crowd who noticed as quite odd. The men whose task it was to prepare the place of execution were busy as could be. A cacophony of shouts, taunts, and obscene laughter grew gradually louder as they scurried around the small hilltop preparing the great cross on which Philip was to hang mercilessly until dead. The apostle could hear every insult they were casting like stones, but he did not appear to be affected by their hateful words. He did not even seem frightened before the grim certainty of the execution awaiting him. He merely took one great and deep breath after another as he watched the scene unfold before him.

"Philip," a strong and compassionate voice uttered from somewhere both near and far.

His heart leaped with joy and anticipation as the voice penetrated him to the bone. As if instantly transported with no kind of conveyance, Philip was suddenly reclining at table in a dimly lit room. His awestruck eyes darted round the table as he recognized his old friends, many of whom he had not seen in years. So many wonderful things they had seen together! All because the Lord had called them to his side. Why had he done it? Why had he called each one of them in particular? Philip had never really felt that he understood why such simple

and ordinary men should be preferred to more likely candidates, but the Lord's will was unquestionably wise.

Philip was shocked at the vividness of this memory. It revealed itself to him like a treasured heirloom brought out for cherishing after many years of safekeeping. The Lord was speaking about his Father. From the first moments of his acquaintance he had always done so. Philip listened intently, remembering each detail precisely as it had been that night.

"In my Father's house there are many rooms," said the Lord. "If this were not so, would I have told you that I am going to prepare a place for you? My friends, I will come to you once more, and I will take you to myself, that where I am you may be also. And where I am going, you know the way."

They were all amazed at his words and pondered them deeply as they looked in his eyes through the dim candlelight. Thomas' words broke the silence, "Lord, how can we know the way if we do not know where you are going?"

The Lord spoke solemnly and clearly, "I am the way, and the truth, and the life." He looked slowly around the table, gazing at each one of them. "No one comes to the Father except through me. If you know me, you surely know my Father as well. Truly I say to you, from now on you know him and have seen him."

Philip now spoke, "Lord, show us the Father... that will be enough for us." His anticipation and

curiosity seemed as strong as it had been that night and the request had practically burst forth from his lips.

Jesus paused for a few moments before replying. His eyes never left Philip's.

"Philip, my friend. Do you still not understand? How long have I been with you, and you still do not know me?" He paused again briefly before continuing.

"If you have seen me, you have seen the Father. How can you say, 'Show us the Father', Philip? I am always in the Father, and the Father is always in me. He and I are one, bound forever by the Spirit of Love whom we share."

None of them spoke, so rapt were they in the Lord's every word. Whenever he spoke to them his words seemed to be both near and far. They raised up those who heard them to something beyond comprehension, and yet they were intimate, close to you and penetrating your heart.

"Truly, truly, I say to you," the Lord continued once more, "he who believes in me will also do works like I do. Indeed, he will do even greater works, because I am soon going to the Father. Whatever you ask in my name, friends, I will do it. I will do what you ask in my name so that the Father may be glorified in the Son."

In the blink of an eye, Philip was back in Hierapolis, now grasped fiercely by the arms and forced forward to the dreadful scene finally prepared for him. The table of death was now set,

and its attendants stood by in eager anticipation of serving up Philip to death as though he were some kind of delicacy.

They threw him onto the cross so roughly that he gasped with pain. Dizzy and disoriented from their incessant blows to his head and body, he did not even notice the nails they had hastily grabbed before they began to drive them through his palms. Philip wept uncontrollably as the nails plunged ever deeper. As they swiftly hoisted him up for all to see, his blood flowed freely down the cross and pooled on the rocky ground below. Jeers and laughter rose up from the crowd to his ears, but he was rapidly losing focus as first minutes and then hours dragged on at a miserably slow pace. He was beyond weary, his throat dry, body soaked with sweat and blood.

Amidst the agony his tortured mind had somehow anchored itself on the Lord's words yet again: "Ask in my name..." He closed his eyes and gathered all of himself as best he could.

"Please, Lord..." he managed to utter, "Take me home..."

The instant he spoke the words his eyes beheld an incredible sight. Walking through the massive throng, undetected by a single person but Philip, the Lord approached. He stepped forward with such grace and peace that Philip's tears of pain were transformed into tears of exultation. Now at the foot of Philip's cross, the Lord looked up at him, stretched out his hand and smiled.

"Philip, my dear friend," he said softly. "The time has come. "

CHAPTER THREE

Matthew

Matthew's heart raced so intensely that it caused his stomach to churn. Though his prayers were ceaselessly rising up to the heavens, the feelings of fear and distress gathered over him like storm clouds. Terrible shouts from the men who were hunting him echoed off the mud-brick buildings and he kept very still, not even daring to breathe too loudly.

It was nearly dark out now. The sun was setting as though none of Matthew's dire situation mattered to it in the slightest; as though this were just like any other day. It did not seem fair. He almost felt as though nature itself should recognize the gravity of this moment, but he dismissed such fancies as quickly as they had arisen in his troubled mind.

Matthew did not like hiding, yet he was not sure what else to do. He had reacted instinctively when he heard they were coming. This day's arrival had not surprised him, for it was only a matter of time. What had the others thought and felt when this day had found them? Had they been as terrified as he now felt? Matthew ruminated over this question relentlessly as he dared to peer around the corner for a moment.

No one there. But he could hear them, and he could sense the danger in his bones. *Am I a coward?* The question kept leaping into his mind every few minutes. The knot in his stomach twisted and would not relent. What made one man a coward and another a hero? How could one person summon the courage to stand tall and unwavering as the beasts raged toward him with open jaws while another man turned at the first hint of danger and ran for shelter?

"He went this way! Over here!" shouted a familiar voice.

Matthew kept impossibly still and silent. The voice belonged to a young soldier Matthew had occasionally encountered. This man's name was Genet, captain of the guard of King Hertacus. Hertacus had listened to Matthew's preaching with great interest for a time. But his lust for his own niece had prompted a sharp rebuke from Matthew and the king now sought his blood. Genet was dispatched to find the troublemaking preacher, this foreign pest, and put him to a swift end.

Now the end is surely near, thought Matthew. He peered once more around the corner. Still no one in sight. But he heard them searching, shouting, invading homes. House after house sent up shocked outbursts of anger or fear or confused frustration. Suddenly, the overturning of a table in one home filled the cold night air with the echo of scattered coins as they cascaded to the floor. Matthew's heart seemed to stop in an instant as a distant memory

emerged round him. It all felt so real, so tangible, as though it were something he could pick up and hold, cupped in his hands.

Matthew saw himself sitting at a money-changing table, a much younger man. Younger indeed, but also foolish, and selfish, and altogether empty. He had not loved the Romans, far from it. But neither did he love his own people. That was a lifetime ago. Had he ever truly been this man, this "Levi"? Surely he had. Yet it was difficult to accept sometimes. Nothing could have ever been the same after that day. The Lord changed everything.

Matthew watched the familiar and yet still incredulous scene unfold. Young Levi sat engrossed in his business. He did not care about the neighbors he cheated. He did not care about the Romans, the religious leaders, or even himself, really. The truth was that Matthew, as Levi, had not really cared about anything. He worked as a tax collector because he was good at it and it was reliable, predictable, something he felt he could control. Deep down he was a man beset by fear. But his lifelong fear of poverty was not so much a fear of needing money yet having none. It was a fear of needing the help of others and having it willingly offered. Levi feared relationship. In a word, he feared love. There was something awesome and awful and terrifying and demanding and total about love, and thus Levi could not bear to even look in love's direction. That is until the day Love came by his booth and looked at him.

Matthew would never forget the Lord's eyes. It was hard to describe them. No, it was impossible to describe them. They saw everything. They pierced you the whole way through and they left no corner in the shadows. Yet they were never intrusive. They journeyed nowhere you yourself did not consent to let them go, for they were filled with such peace and sincerity you could not imagine refusing their request to enter into the truest, deepest, most secret sanctuary of your heart. The Lord smiled. Levi, now Matthew, eyes welling with tears, merely smiled in return.

The scene faded from view as Matthew became vaguely aware of a hard, cold, tight pain in his back and chest. He did not look down, for his eyes were still locked in the love-effusing gaze that had transformed him entirely those many years ago. He could hear shouting and the crescendo of clamoring voices as a crowd began to surround him. The feeling in Matthew's torso went numb as Genet withdrew his blade and pushed the perishing apostle's body to the sandy ground of the alley. Some in the crowd began to throw stones at him, but Matthew's attention was elsewhere.

A figure, somehow unnoticed by the others, approached Matthew. In an instant, the fading man found himself in the arms of the One he had once feared to embrace; the One, rather, whose eternal embrace he himself had feared to receive. Once Matthew had abandoned that fear he had never been the same, for now he loved all, he embraced all,

and he sought out all men and women with the call that beckoned them to come to the Lord. Matthew closed his eyes in the tender grip of the Lord and entered into the glory.

CHAPTER FOUR

Peter

Peter could not help but smile, even if only so slightly. The present circumstances hardly called for such a thing, yet he was finding himself mysteriously led to a place that was far beyond his circumstances. His heart and mind had spirited him away for a moment to a place that felt both familiar and foreign.

That place was the Sea of Galilee. *How many days and nights did we spend there?* It was impossible to guess. He had fished its depths for what seemed like a lifetime, and indeed that was now a lifetime ago. He had been another man entirely. Rude. Stubborn. Clumsy on occasion. He had also been impatient and impulsive. Nobody expected very much of Peter and, truth be told, that was just fine with him.

But the Lord had changed everything, and from the moment he got into Peter's boat nothing would ever be the same. That was just what he did. He came to all people, right to their boats, their shops, their tax collecting booths. He met everyone eye to eye. The Lord was the Great Fisher of Men, and he never ceased to seek them all out, even Peter.

His focus was momentarily broken by a sharp jolt of pain, iron shackles cruelly yanking him forward. The guards who held onto the other ends of his chains continued their mockery. They tugged and pulled, spit and cursed. The regular blows to his face caused his blood to mingle ever more profusely with the sweat dripping from his brow.

Weary but lucid, Peter moved onward. *What had Paul called us?* he pondered. *Slaves of Christ?* He managed a grin for another brief moment before the guard on his left took notice and struck him hard on his left ear. Peter winced, but he resolved more than ever to endure. He had to see this through to the end.

Suddenly the journey from his cell to Nero's arena on the Vatican Hill came to an alarmingly abrupt end. They exited a dimly lit tunnel into the shimmering June sun. The dusty air was hot, and the sand was hotter. A hard shove sent Peter into an awkward and terrible fall. The chains dug in more deeply than ever and course, scorching sand now began to cling to his bloody, broken body. All around him the crowds roared, but the single tear that rolled gently down his bruised cheek was shed for love's sake, not for fear. *My brothers and sisters,* he thought prayerfully, *will you not let go of hatred and be free? Will you not see what God has in store for those who love him?*

Two guards grasped his arms and hurried him forward to the wooden beams.

"I come here at last," Peter said in a low whisper.

The altar of sacrifice - the same one that awaited the Lord! He could feel the dread welling up inside him. It was like an old, far too familiar voice, beckoning to him. This voice was his old enemy. It had won him over before countless times, none of them so shameful as the night on which he had denied the Lord three times. He vowed never to let the voice seduce him again, and he knew these next moments would prove to be his final test.

They thrust him down hard upon the large wooden cross beams, kicking him and cursing him more rabidly. The throngs of people in their seats above chanted and shouted, worshiping the wicked scene below as though it were some divine liturgy. Peter tried to breathe slowly, whispering the Lord's name over and over again as he begged for the courage and the endurance to not forsake him in these last moments.

The hammer struck hard. Peter could not keep from crying out in most gruesome agony. As the nails plunged deeper and deeper into his flesh he was most deeply wounded not by his own excruciating pain, but by the realization of what the Lord had felt in these moments. Clang! The hammer sang its savage song. Clang! The nails sank their devilish teeth into their prey seeking to devour all joy and peace, even the memories of such things.

It was in the bleakest depths of this affliction, when the poisonous voice enticed him most intensely to abandon all hope that it happened. Peter could see him. The Lord was there - he was right

there! And through unthinkable torment he was whisked away once more to the sea. What a terrifying storm it had been! Peter remembered it well, for in all his years on the sea he had never seen anything like it. Now he was there again, the others with him in the boat clinging to life and to one another. But Peter was looking out to sea. The Lord stood there a ways off, and he stood on the water! The waves crashed around him and the wind howled ferociously, but he never moved. He just stood there with an astonishingly calm expression on his face and his strong hand outstretched to Peter.

The others were stunned and, for a moment, speechless as Peter began to climb out of the boat and onto the angry waves. He ignored their mounting desperate shouts to stay as he ventured out onto the deep stepping cautiously as though walking on glass. To his bewilderment, the waves held him up. Or rather no, he corrected his old memory: *The Lord held me up!* Peter did not look down. At first he found that he simply could not take his eyes off the Lord. His face filled Peter with the confidence to go on, to keep trudging forward in this impossible trek across the chaos. *How was this possible? This was truly unheard of! Could it be a dream? How long could this continue? Could this continue?*

Gradually the fear and doubt began to encircle him. Peter sensed a desire to break the gaze rising up in him like the waves upon which he tread. Finally in his weakness, overcome by this urge, Peter looked away for the first time. The instant that

happened, he rapidly plunged into the churning darkness.

The memory broke and he was again fully present in the arena. Peter felt a surge of newfound strength. *Not this time! Not here.* Steadfastly fixed to the wood of his cross, the guards prepared to raise Peter up. Somehow he managed to gather enough air in his lungs to abruptly cry out.

"Not like my Lord! I am not worthy! Upside down! Up...side...down!"

The guards roared with careless laughter and did as the old man asked. It made no difference to them.

He was fading now, his vision blurred by dirt and sand, blood and sweat. He struggled to breathe as an entire lifetime raced through his mind. Then in a final grace filled moment, he fixed his dying eyes on those of his beloved Lord. Surrounded by the most treacherous and raging sea of his life, Peter refused the final temptation to doubt, to fear, to lose hope. He was going to his Lord, and this time he would not be swallowed up by the darkness. With his last breath, he uttered the words he had shouted those many years ago.

"Lord... Save me!"

The Lord smiled, and Peter was born into eternal life.

CHAPTER FIVE

Paul

P aul awoke before the day did. He rubbed his old, weary eyes, yawned, and scratched the top of his bald head. *Today*, he thought. *After all this time, it is finally here.* Paul surveyed the tiny cell. It was dark, damp, and the horrible smell had not grown more bearable despite the time he had spent here. Regardless, he prayed. *Thank you, Lord. How many of my brothers and sisters have no shelter at all? Even this prison lies within your will, and you know far better than I how much worse I deserve.*

Noise in the corridor began to swell as the jailers approached his door. Keys clanked and clanged as they were jostled into the lock. Paul heard one of the jailers swear as he muscled the old iron door open. Two men entered his musty cell. He looked at them both, gazing into their eyes as he had become accustomed to do with everyone. It was a searching look, one that could only be made by someone who had nothing to hide anymore - someone who had been entirely transformed by grace. Many on the receiving end of this gaze found it uncomfortable. Some even became angry. Today, for these guards, it was the latter.

"Get up!" the larger of the two shouted at the apostle.

Paul obeyed, but it was too slow for the guards. The one who had shouted at Paul grabbed him like a vice at the elbow and wrenched him up. They swiftly shackled his hands and pushed him toward the doorway.

"Move!"

Paul shuffled down the corridor as the sounds from other cells perforated the air around him. Some cells produced bitter weeping, others shouts of pain and terror. Still others amplified the cries of men driven mad by thoughts of the death that awaited them, the same death to which Paul now marched with an uncanny peace and resolution. Those who glimpsed him sweeping past their cell could not make sense of his tranquility.

The march from Paul's cell to Tre Fontane, the place where he was to die, took quite some time. Along the way, a passing stranger or group would occasionally spit on him or throw a rock his way. Some missed - others did not. Every so often a passerby would look on him with pity and he would look back with merciful love. Paul loved and blessed them all, friends and enemies alike. Eventually, the execution site was reached and a small crowd of a dozen or so had assembled there. The guards led Paul up to a small platform where a centurion awaited alongside the sword-bearing executioner.

Paul was praying all the while, so immersed in prayer that the order of execution being read aloud

was practically imperceptible to him. The centurion finished the proclamation and rolled up the scroll. He motioned for the guards to lead Paul to the short column to which he would be bound. The condemned man glanced at the crowd. One face caught his attention and his heart leaped with the love of the Lord himself. It was Julius of the Cohort Augusta, the centurion who had been Paul's jailer and escort to Rome from Adramyttium. Though a loyal Roman soldier, Julius had shown kindness to Paul during that treacherous journey. The executioner now stood beside Paul, ready to carry out his duty. But Paul's heart and mind were many miles distant, on the island of Malta.

It was winter. Paul sat alone on a large rock outcropping as the serene waves spoke in whispers to an attentive shore. They were far more peaceful than their angry, vengeful sisters who had torn Paul's ship to pieces on the open sea. The voyage had been truly shuddersome, but Paul knew they would be spared. An angel had revealed the news to him at the bleakest moment, and this hope had sustained him and the others.

Someone drew near. Paul turned to see Julius, his jailer, descending to the shore from the house of Publius, the island's chief who had graciously allowed them to winter on Malta.

"Good evening, friend!" Paul called out to him.

"Are you not cold?" Julius replied, surprised that Paul seemed perfectly content despite the bitter wind and the icy surf.

"When you've been shipwrecked as often as me, you grow accustomed, I suppose."

Julius nodded, amused. He sat next to Paul and the two of them took in the sunset. Huge clouds played with the light turning it pink and orange, then purple and blue. Silence. The rhythmic waves were so steady that the two men no longer noticed them. It was Julius who eventually broke the silence.

"I don't understand you, old man."

Paul turned to him and gave him that penetrating look. He said nothing.

"You don't seem like much of a threat to me. Your words are of peace and forgiveness and hope. You are kind to all you meet. You speak boldly, yet not to injure."

Paul smiled and shook his head looking back to the open sea.

"If only you had known me then. Before the Lord picked me up in all my murderous fury and threw me to the ground, blind."

Julius marveled at him. He stood up and advanced a few paces toward the sea. He seemed distressed, unsettled. A few moments later he spun around.

"You know you will die, Paul! You are to die for all this. It is set!"

Paul arose and slowly came down to where Julius stood. Waves crashed harmlessly nearby spraying them with frothy foam.

"You don't understand, Julius," Paul leaned in very close and spoke in almost a whisper. "You see,

I am already dead. I carry Christ's death in me always."

Julius stared back incredulously and shook his head. Paul now came eye to eye with him and placed his hand on his shoulder. It was the hand of a man who had suffered much.

"But that isn't the end of the story, my son. He is alive, Julius! The Lord lives! He suffered death for *every* man, to set *all* men free. He calls to you as well, but you don't yet wish to hear him."

At this, Julius angrily grasped Paul's hand and pushed it away. He spun around and made for the village, but as he stormed off, he heard Paul speak further.

"Perhaps you *have* heard his voice, but you fear to listen to him."

"I fear nothing!" Julius retorted with a quick glance over his shoulder.

"Death!" Paul's word was like an arrow piercing Julius' armor. He froze in his tracks and then turned to face the old apostle.

"You fear death, don't you? The unknown? The great abyss opening beneath your feet and swallowing you up whole? You always have."

Julius could not so much as budge. His breath had grown shallow and he stood rigid as a corpse. Paul was now only a few feet away from him. The old, steady yet weak hand rested once more on his shoulder.

"Do not be afraid, my son. I preach Christ, and him crucified. He came down into that abyss, the

one you tremble to even imagine. He waits for you there, for we must all go into that darkest of nights. But we need no longer fear. He waits for us, the Light of the World, who will draw his children out of the darkness and into the endless day."

Paul patted Julius' shoulder and began the walk back to Publius' house. The centurion remained by the shore through the night.

Now standing in the small crowd at Tre Fontane, he wept as he and Paul gazed at one another. Paul smiled at him as he prayed. *Oh Lord! What about him? What of your Julius? Will he finally hear your voice? Can I offer my present sufferings for him, this last moment, in the hope that he might embrace you at last?*

No sooner had Paul uttered these words than the executioner, receiving the centurion's command, raised the gleaming blade high in the morning sun. The light reflected off it and shone on a face Paul had not yet seen. He shouted out in spirited delight. *Lord!* The Lord stood just behind Julius. He smiled the smile of heaven itself, the smile of all holy men and women through the ages.

"Yes, Paul," he heard in his very soul, "Julius will live."

Paul's eyes, once blind but now filled with refulgent light, closed in joy as the sword descended.

CHAPTER SIX

Andrew

"We have found the Messiah!" Those had been the excited words Andrew shouted to his brother Peter. Decades had passed since then, and Andrew found it ever more difficult to remember what life had been like before the Lord had come. Nothing could be the same after you met him. His very presence seemed to bring a person to a decision point, for no one could merely brush him to the side. Andrew saw this play out so many times he had lost count.

Andrew had long since come to think of himself as the Lord's introducer. He learned many years ago that God had given him this talent which carried with it a twofold character. He introduced people to the Lord and, in a sense, he introduced the Lord to them. He was an apostle who saw his particular gift to be one of invitation and greeting, and he was immeasurably grateful to God for calling him to this life, even if it meant enduring what was about to come.

The crowd gathering around him was filled with conflicted faces. Some seethed with anger and hatred, thirsty for the blood of this troublemaker before them. Others looked on with a curious

indifference to Andrew's fate. Still others wore expressions of confused and fearful discontent with the situation at hand, yet these persons would not likely find the courage to stand with either Andrew's accusers or his defenders if they were pressured to do so. Fearful self-preservation was their guiding drive. It seemed that in the final estimation, Andrew had no friends and an abundance of enemies.

He felt a sorrowful love for the poor souls who had allowed themselves to be so engulfed in the flames of hatred that they could no longer feel the heat. He pitied the lukewarm who were so dulled by their frequent sins that they could be so genuinely careless, truly caring for nothing of substance any longer. He pitied the fearful ones who would never take a stand so long as a terrible shadow dominated the little world they had built round themselves and beyond which they refused to gaze. *This is why you came*, he thought, *and all I ask of you now is for the chance to introduce them to you this last time.*

"Well?" shouted the magistrate, festooned about with all the trim and regalia of his office. "Do you recant this ridiculous doctrine? Or will you not yield?"

Andrew did not reply for what seemed like a long time. Finally, as the judge was about to once more demand a response, Andrew spoke softly but with unshakable conviction.

"How can I do what you require of me, my lord? These proceedings rest upon a great deception. I

stand accused of heresy, of preaching a mere man as God. But this is not the truth."

The noise of the crowd subsided as people eagerly hushed one another. They were curious to hear what he had to say, and Andrew continued.

"This man, Christ Jesus, I knew as intimately as one can know a friend. Indeed, I knew him more intimately than anyone else in my life, for *I was known* so perfectly by him. He looked into my eyes not as one man to another, not even as a dear friend or closest kin. When he looked into my eyes, he did so as the one who fashioned them. His gaze pierced and it pierces still the very heart, for he is the maker of all men's hearts, the great artisan who shapes all creation and who breathes into all living things the spirit of life. He descended into the deep so as to raise up that which has fallen beyond all reaching but his own. And so I, one of the lost ones whom he found there, have set out to tell men this glorious news! Once I said that we had found him. In these last days I see that it is he who has found us. He finds all men who are humble enough to let themselves be found. Alas, many prefer the bitter and barren darkness. Which kind of man I wonder, my lord, will you decide to be?"

The crowd murmured in utter shock, aghast at this foreign peasant's gall. Did he not understand what would be done to him should he finally refuse to desist this madness? The magistrate glared at Andrew with an expression of rapidly vanishing patience.

"How dare you lecture me!" he fumed. "It is you who are on trial here, not me! You speak as though you were some great teacher, some holy man of great repute and boundless wisdom. But I see through you, you charlatan! You self-righteous little fiend! You seek to unravel our entire society with your talk of this god-man, this impossible fantasy wherein weakness is touted as strength and death is destroyed by death! Nonsense! Blasphemous insanity!"

The magistrate was standing now, clearly shaking with rage, though he quickly sought to collect himself and to salvage some appearance of objectivity before it was consumed entirely by his fury and the mob's relentless thirst for blood. Andrew breathed slowly and deeply, silently standing before the magistrate while the mob beheld him with contempt.

"I am no great man," he began. "I am a fisherman, my lord. It has been my trade since I was a boy. It was not my will to leave my boat and my nets - it was the will of God. He called to us, my brother and me. He said, 'Come... and I will make you fishers of men.' I am just a poor and simple man; a man who offers the only thing he can offer to everyone he meets."

"Which is?" demanded the magistrate impatiently.

"Him," Andrew replied, slowly pointing to the edge of the crowd. Countless faces turned to behold

whoever this strange man was indicating. But they saw no one. Only Andrew could see him.

"Enough!" shouted the magistrate. "Take him away! His sentence is death!"

The guards took hold of Andrew and dragged him fiercely to a sheer precipice overlooking the sea. There they hastily fastened him to a solitary X-shaped cross, the widely spread planks stretching his crushed body to an intolerable level of pain. Minutes passed like hours, hours like days. Yet as people passed by the hideous sight, they were shocked to hear not the agonizing cries of a tortured man, but rather a soft cadence that sounded like a lullaby.

"We have found him... We have found him... O Morning Star, Dawn of Ages long foretold! The One whose shadow my people chased has shown himself to us at last! My Lord, my Love! My Rock, my Guide! I see you! I see your face! Receive your lowly servant!"

At long last the Great Morning dawned over the pounding waves, and swept Andrew's pain away forevermore.

CHAPTER SEVEN

Nathanael

"Can anything good come from Nazareth?" Had he really said those words to Philip? Nathanael tried with all his might to remember, rather, to relive that day in his mind.

The pain at present, however, was truly unbearable. His tormentors worked their foul deeds of cruelty and the agony pierced him to the core. He knew he must now turn every last corner of his world over to the Lord, for no human effort alone could withstand such torture. All was in the Lord's hands. It always was.

Searing pangs swept through his whole body like an earthquake rushing mercilessly along its path of destruction. He bit down hard, clenched his shaking fists, and tried his very best not to cry out. *Lord!* He prayed in his mind. *Be with me! Give me whatever I need!*

With that he felt a very strange thing take place. It was as though Nathanael was in two places at once. On the one hand, he was still strapped to the table and being treated with unspeakable wickedness. And yet, he also found himself sitting under a fig tree on a beautiful, sun bathed day outside Bethsaida in Galilee. He knew this place

well. But how could this be? He felt both the unbridled infliction of pain and the tranquility of basking in the peace of his younger years under this, his favorite tree.

So strange, he thought to himself. As if in the haze of a dream which cannot be fully made out, Nathanael gradually came to the realization that he was somehow observing a memory. He could see himself as a young man, his youthful self not yet weathered by the winds of time and age, but himself all the same.

Young Nathanael sat under the tree in peaceful relaxation. People walked about nearby, coming and going about their business and paying no particular attention to him. He did not mind it much, for Nathanael had never considered himself a social person. He tended to keep to himself for the most part. He had few friends to speak of, Philip being one of them. It was Philip who now approached his spot under the tree, and he looked as though something urgent was happening. Nathanael sat up suddenly and looked inquisitively at his friend.

"What is this all about?" Nathanael wondered aloud as his friend rushed toward him. Philip was, after all, not known to be one who was easily excited unless the situation greatly warranted it.

"Bartholomew!" cried Philip.

Nathanael cringed at the nickname. Today was one of those days where "Talmai's Son" wanted a little more of the fig tree's shadow than his father's. He chose to ignore Philip.

"Nathanael!" Philip shouted more intensely. He had nearly reached the tree now.

"What is it?" asked Nathanael impatiently. "You don't run very often so I imagine this is pretty important!"

"We have found him!" exclaimed Philip.

"You've found who?" replied Nathanael.

"The one we've been waiting for! The one Moses spoke of! The one whom the prophets foretold!" Philip could hardly contain himself. He was panting and covered with sweat from the unpracticed exertion.

"What are you talking about?" Nathanael asked in a skeptical tone.

"The Messiah! He is here! Our savior is here!" Philip was jumping up and down with childlike gleefulness. Some passersby looked their way and Nathanael, somewhat embarrassed, spoke more quietly while trying to calm his friend.

"Who, Philip? Who are you talking about?"

"Jesus!" replied Philip. "Jesus of Nazareth, son of Joseph, the carpenter!"

Nathanael scoffed without a moment's hesitation. "Nazareth!" he retorted indignantly. "Can anything good come from Nazareth?"

The memory flickered momentarily as the old man lying on the execution table shuddered. The most intense throes of agony he had ever felt coursed through his whole body. He cried out this time. He could not help it. But he gathered himself and was quickly back at the tree. He felt ashamed for

those words. He had for years. Nazareth. *I never knew*, he thought. *I never knew the treasure you concealed, Nazareth. Did you? I joined in the mockery, the disdain for your sons and daughters because I loved my own pride more than my neighbor*. His young self stood there in disbelief and arrogant dismissal.

Philip, not at all dissuaded, laughed at his skeptical friend. Doubtless, Nathanael's insult was not unexpected.

"Come and see," was all Philip said.

Nathanael agreed, for in truth he was curious. Not curious to see if this Jesus was truly the promised Holy One of Israel, but curious to see how this crazy Nazorean was able to convince someone like Philip to believe his claims. *This will be interesting*, he thought to himself in amused anticipation.

Not desiring to run, Nathanael walked casually behind his enthusiastic friend. After a few minutes they could make out a small group of people ahead, a half dozen or so. As the two friends drew near the group parted somewhat and a man began to approach them. The instant their eyes met, there was a stirring in Nathanael's soul he could never quite describe.

Smiling broadly, the stranger said, "Behold! Here is a true Israelite, in whom there is no deceit!"

"How do you know me?" asked Nathanael, taken aback by a strange sense stirring within.

"I saw you," the man replied. "I saw you under the fig tree."

Then something profound happened, for without speaking another audible word, the man's voice continued in a strange, clear, and peaceful tone. Nathanael could hear him, and yet no one else seemed to.

"Do not be afraid, Bartholomew! I know you because no one can know you better than I. You are a word spoken by Another. My Father in Heaven has dreamt you, spoken you through me, and He has sent me to you now by the breath of His Spirit. I have come for you, cherished one. Will you come and follow me?"

Nathanael was speechless. Could this really be happening? Who was *he* that God would ask him, invite him of all people? He felt entirely unworthy, unqualified, and most of all, ashamed of his sins. He was surely unsuited for anything God could possibly ask of him. But so too was he lifted up by a new stillness and peace within. He could not stop staring into the Lord's eyes. He knew in an instant that he could never turn away from those eyes, those eyes which contained every mystery, every answer, everything he could ever hope or dream.

"Rabbi!" he cried, nearly shocking himself with vigor and jubilation. "You are the Son of God - the King of Israel!"

The Lord smiled, never taking his eyes off Nathanael.

"You will see greater things than these," he said, reaching his hand forward to greet him.

Once more, the agony of the moment abruptly wrenched Nathanael from the vision. He knew that there were only moments left now. The cruel men laughed and mocked him as he faded, but they were not his focus - the Lord was.

"You've come for me!" the poor dying man said with tear drenched eyes.

He struggled with his last strength to stretch out his shackled, bloody hands as far as they could reach.

"Can anything good come from Nazareth?" the Lord calmly, almost amusingly asked.

Nathanael smiled.

"Yes..." he whispered, the final word from his lips.

CHAPTER EIGHT

Thomas

Thomas closed his eyes and breathed more deeply. A slight grin appeared on his weary face as he chased the memories, so many long years removed and yet so vivid. It was not overly difficult to find them, and every time he did it was as though they became real once more.

He had not been able to bear it the day they had taken the Lord away. His world completely collapsed when he heard the dreadful news that they had crucified him. *He is dead! Dead? How could he be dead? How could this have happened? How could the Lord be gone?* But there were other questions, too. *How could I have abandoned him in his hour of need? How could he have abandoned us after such displays of power and might? What am I, what are any of us to do now?* So many questions and not an answer in sight.

Thomas wandered aimlessly in the days that followed. He walked and walked. He tried to pray but, more often than not, no words came. He gave some money to a beggar. He helped an old woman who had dropped her things in a crowded marketplace. He gave some bread to a hungry orphan. But no matter where he went during those

three days, he could not stop repeating those painful questions in his troubled heart and mind.

On the third day, he summoned up the courage and went out to the place where the Lord had died. The instant he crested the hill, Thomas burst into tears. Everywhere he looked he could see the traces of what had taken place there. Blood still saturated the ground in several places. A discarded heap of thorns lay a few feet away, the remnant of the humiliating crown they had forced him to wear. And just beyond this, he found one of the enormous nails that had been driven through the Lord's hands or his feet. Thomas buckled as he clutched the nail tightly, sobbing uncontrollably atop Golgotha until the sun began to sink low on the horizon.

He took his time that evening. He was not particularly pressed to return to the others. After all, what was the point? What would they do now? What was to become of them? More questions. He had scarcely reached the door when he heard a commotion coming from inside the house. Rapid-paced voices, thrilled yet hushed, resounded from within the locked upper room. Thomas knocked, and they went silent.

"It's me," Thomas said, "I'm back."

"Thomas!" shouted several of the others as they threw open the door.

Their mood took him by surprise. They looked like giddy children, yet so too did they seem to be in a state of awestruck wonder. They all spoke at once, rushing to share with him their astonishing news.

Thomas was quickly overwhelmed by the clamor and he motioned in desperation.

"Slow down! I can't understand you! Peter - what has happened?" Thomas shouted to the weathered fisherman.

Peter was seated on a small rug in the corner of the room. He was the only one who had not been speaking along with the others. He turned slowly toward Thomas as the others suddenly grew silent. A joy-filled smile Thomas had never before witnessed beamed across Peter's sea-worn face like the dawn. He rose and approached his confused friend.

"He is risen, Thomas," said Peter with deepest conviction.

"What?" replied Thomas in a daze.

"He lives!" cried Philip.

"The Lord has risen from the dead!" exclaimed Simon.

They all joined in once more in a cascade of affirmation, leaping for joy and filled with wonder.

"What are you saying?!" rebuked Thomas, stunned beyond all measure. "What do you mean he is risen from the dead?"

John explained to him at length what had transpired, how the Lord, though the doors had been locked, appeared in their midst that very afternoon. The others could hardly contain their excitement. Like young boys trying to convey urgent news, they practically stumbled over one another as they told him the whole story.

It was far too much for Thomas. He could hear no more of this. The Lord had been ripped from him and he now felt completely empty inside. He was hollow. It was as though his heart had beat its last and would remain still in his chest forever hence.

"No!" Thomas cried out, startling the others and himself to an extent. "I cannot... Unless I see him with my own eyes - unless I put my own hands into his wounds, I will not believe!"

With this outburst, he rushed from their presence distraught and greatly troubled.

The next days came and went without significance. Before long Thomas found himself once more with the others. It was then that the astounding thing that had happened to them finally happened to him. *He is here!* The risen Lord stood in their midst, shining like a thousand suns yet somehow calming them all with infinite tenderness. Thomas stared at him for untold moments that seemed to span a lifetime.

"Thomas," began the Lord, "here I am. You see me, do you not?"

Thomas stood frozen, mouth agape in astonishment.

"Come. Put your hands in my hands. Touch my side. See the price I willingly paid for you, my dear friend..."

Thomas fell to his knees, tears welling up so much that he could barely see through them. But he knew in his heart that he no longer needed to see anything. He believed with every fiber of his being.

He understood now, and he would never doubt again.

"My Lord… and my *God!*"

Now, opening his aged eyes, eyes that had seen so many incredible things in the years since the Lord had first called him, Thomas stepped forward into the garish light. The journey would finally end here, today. The journey had taken him from Israel to India. His work was now done, the seeds planted. Though evil would rage against it, the tree would grow - of that, he had no doubt.

Sudden flashes of pain wracked his body as the spears pierced him all over. Thomas wobbled, dazed and rapidly losing balance, but the torment began to fade as quickly as it had come. As the light dwindled, his once doubtful eyes beheld their final sight: the eternally pierced hands of his Lord grasping his own and clutching them tightly, never to let go.

CHAPTER NINE

James the Lesser

"You will do as you are told!" shrieked the high priest. "This blasphemy ends now! Today!" He was shaking with rage as he pounded the table between him and the man in chains who stood silent and unruffled. Their eyes locked for an instant and James could see that the high priest's fury ran deep.

"I must speak the truth. I will never do otherwise. You must do your duty as you see it, as must I," James said slowly, as directly as possible.

A hideous grin formed on the high priest's lips and he nodded slowly.

"We shall see," he replied.

Signaling the Temple guards with a mere wave of his hand, the high priest stared once more into James' eyes. He saw resolution, no chance of a change of mind. Such a fool. How could it be that after all these years they were still dealing with this ridiculous cult? Worse - how had they swayed the hearts and minds of so many followers? How could anyone fall for such nonsense? "He is risen!" They proclaimed it incessantly. They spoke of this crucified nobody from Galilee of all places as though he had actually conquered death! This was madness,

a fairy tale created by this band of uneducated miscreants for attention and nothing more. They could not possibly believe such things. If they did not, they were the worst kind of blasphemers and false prophets. If they actually did, they were insane and dangerous. Either way, the high priest knew that they had to be stopped, no matter the cost.

The guards seized James and pulled him swiftly from the room. Pushing and shoving him as they marched along, James began to pray silently. *My beloved Lord, do not allow me to fail you now.* They moved at an urgent pace through courtyards and down several corridors before reaching a great staircase. It seemed to go on forever. James had always been wary of high places, ever since childhood. He hesitated for a moment and the impatient guards kicked him hard which caused James to lunge forward onto the cold stone stairs. He winced, dazed but not seriously injured.

"Get up! Climb!" they shouted down at him.

James obeyed without quarrel or resistance. He began to ascend the stairs and his mind sought out a specific memory, one he had not revisited for some time but that he knew very well. It was a cool day and the harvest had begun. He was only a boy, though he never could quite remember how old he had been. Ten? Nine perhaps? It did not matter. That day was like so many others at first. James and his brother Jude ran about their village without a care in the world. They played, they fought, they laughed

and explored curious places and things. They soon crossed paths with a group of friends.

"James!" shouted their friend Benjamin. "Look at that!"

Benjamin was pointing up at the corner of a tall building near the edge of the village. James and the others saw it immediately. It was a large birds' nest, astir with boisterous activity. As the boys looked more closely they could see a small songbird that did not look like the others. It was a rare and remarkable shade of blue with white speckles across its back and wings. James had never seen the like, and he was quickly overcome with the urge to try and catch it.

"I can get him," James assured Jude, "I know I can."

"James, don't!" warned his cautious brother.

It was too late. James was already climbing the side of the house. A foothold here, a ledge to grip there. Soon he was on the roof and the boys below goaded him on while looking around with nervous anticipation of being caught. James inched along the rooftop ledge toward the mysterious bird. It hopped to and fro, evidently oblivious to the advancing curious boy.

"Be careful!" shouted Jude. The interruption startled James and he nearly slipped.

"Be quiet!" he shouted back in a raspy voice.

James was so close now. He began to reach out. The strange blue bird froze suddenly and so did James. He held his breath. *I cannot stay here for long,*

he thought. He knew the owner of this house and he knew what the reaction to his rooftop adventure would be. *Now or never!* James stretched out his hand very slowly. *Almost!*

Without warning, the nest exploded. A dozen birds took flight in a wild and furious cloud around James. Thoroughly panicked, he swatted in vain in every direction attempting to scare them off. Before he could comprehend his situation, he knew he was falling. It was so fast. Nothing he could do. His clothes rippled like waves in the wind and the spectators below cried out in terror.

James landed hard. But it was not the ground upon which he collapsed in a heap - it was a person! James collected himself and tried to make sense of it all. He was frightened, winded, and completely disoriented. Then came a familiar voice.

"Are you alright?" The words were filled with concern, yet they were spoken with a sublime stillness.

"What?" James said in a fog, shaking as his chest heaved.

"Are you hurt?" asked the voice.

James looked up for the first time and saw the speaker. It was his cousin Jesus, the son of his uncle Joseph. James began to make sense of everything. Jesus must have caught him, or rather broken his fall in a somewhat clumsy fashion by jumping underneath James as he fell. The timing! A moment later and James would surely have been terribly injured, or worse.

"I'm... I'm fine..." stammered the stunned boy to his savior, but his cousin had turned away slightly and was reaching for something a few feet away.

Meanwhile, the other boys had rushed over and a commotion arose among them. Some were laughing, some calling him lucky, some were shouting at him in anger. Jude said nothing, but the red eyes he tried to hide and the look on his disappointed face said enough. James was ashamed.

But the clamor subsided as their attention shifted to Jesus. He was kneeling on the ground and he had picked up something, cupping it tenderly in his hands. He turned to them all, but he only looked at James as he opened his hands to reveal what they held. It was the bird, its body shattered and lifeless. It must have happened as he swung at the flock in a frightened panic. James' heart sank as he stared at the motionless creature, its beauty forever ruined by his carelessness. He began to weep bitterly.

His cousin spoke with a peace and assurance James did not expect. "Do not fret, cousin." He looked up to the roof. "You went up to *take* something, it's true."

James' shame ran bone deep and the tears showed it to all.

"But I came down," continued Jesus, "to *give everything*."

Suddenly, something like the rushing wind blew round them all and filled the air with a strange and wonderful sound. It was almost like music in their midst that was somehow springing up from a

far-off place. Never taking his eyes off James, Jesus opened his hands once more. James and the others were astonished at what they held. The bird was alive! Its mangled body restored, beautiful and vibrant, singing its song for all to hear. After a few moments it leaped up from the young carpenter's hands and flew high into the midmorning sun.

Standing along the Temple parapet, James gradually returned from the memory. He was so high up now. The faces in the crowd gathered below were barely perceptible. Guards taunted him and the high priest delivered the stern ultimatum.

"Blasphemer!" he spat. "Do you deny this Jesus? What is your answer?"

James looked once more to the sky and drew a deep breath. As he did, he saw a magnificent blue bird with white speckles across its back and wings flying freely above the Temple courtyard. James gasped and shook with emotion.

"Never," he said with unmistakable finality.

They pushed him over the edge. James plummeted down and down, falling forever from the towering heights. Yet as the whole world flew past him, he was not afraid. No terror gripped him for he knew what awaited him at the end. He could see clearly the end of this final fall below. The Lord, his beloved cousin and savior, stood looking up with arms outstretched and strong, pierced hands reaching to catch him.

CHAPTER TEN

Matthias

He was dizzy, and it was hard to make anything out. Matthias blinked several times in an effort to focus, but it did not help. He looked around on the ground for a few moments before he saw it, the stone that had struck him so hard in the head. The cutthroat throng circled in closer and closer now, and everyone had a stone in his hand. Some men tossed theirs up and down in the palms of their hands with an air of perverse pleasure over the scene about to unfold. *Don't condemn them!* Matthias shouted the words in his mind. *They need the Lord perhaps more than anyone else!*

At that moment, another stone careened through the crowd and crashed into Matthias' right shoulder from behind, its serrated edges tearing his flesh. The impact caused him to cry out and he almost lost his balance. Before he could register the extent of the pain searing throughout his body, two, three, four more large stones pummeled him savagely. One broke his arm below the elbow, another struck him in the head, and the third crippled him at the left knee.

The old apostle collapsed in a gasping heap on the muddy road by the sea. He could no longer

move, at least not willingly. His ever more shattered shell of a body writhed as more stones found their mark. It was harder and harder to breathe now, and Matthias began to grasp for a sturdy memory hoping that it could focus him for these last few moments. He prayed. He prayed hard, and in a flash, he was with the others once more.

He blinked a few times and rubbed his eyes. They were so young! *O, my brothers,* he thought, *how long since we were last together like this!* All of the apostles were gathered: Peter and Andrew, James and John, Phillip, Nathanael, Thomas, Matthew, James and Jude, and Simon. Matthias was back in the moment as if it were all happening again, and what a moment that had been, the day the Eleven drew lots to replace Judas! Matthias could hardly believe it when the lot fell to him. He had never felt worthy to be among their number, not even now. He had been a great sinner - a cheat, a selfish and greedy man. The Lord had brought him into the light. The Lord *was* the Light.

Matthias could never remember exactly how he had first been aware of Jesus and his apostles, but when he heard they were coming through Jericho, he had to at least see the Lord. He had always been a rather short man, so the decision to climb the tree that day amidst the huge crowd was born of necessity. Sure enough, the vantage point was perfect. The moment he saw the Lord, he became a new man. He could not put it into words, but it was as though he saw himself for the first time. He could

no longer hide. No excuses held water. No masks could disguise him from himself, from others, from God. There was no avoiding the truth. He was a sinful man, and he knew it.

That had been the precise instant in which the Lord had stared up at him in the tree as though he were the only person there that day. Suddenly, he called out to him.

"Zaccheus!" Matthias heard his old name once more as the memory ran through his mind. "Come down! I will dine at your house tonight!"

Yet another jagged stone crushed his ribs and he was jarred from the memory. He closed his eyes and made every effort to focus with the last ounce of his strength. *Me... Why did he choose me?* Matthias had pondered this countless times since the lot had fallen to him. So too, as often before, he thought about Judas, the Lord's friend who had betrayed him. *Were we really so different? We both knew how to handle money, and we were quite crafty with it. We loved it. We loved the sense of security it could bring. We loved the influence it seemed to give us, did we not? Surely we both felt the same prideful sense of importance. It kept the fears of nothingness at bay. But it could never really keep the fears away for long, could it?* Matthias had come to that realization the instant the Lord's eyes had locked with his. That was when he had truly died to self. *What was it Paul liked to say about himself, again?* "Last of all, like one untimely born, he appeared to me." How true that had been for Matthias, too!

This would all be over soon. Matthias' thoughts and prayers wandered back to his predecessor one last time. *O, Lord! Did Judas ask you to forgive him before his last breath?* Matthias had wondered this for many years and he hoped so in his heart of hearts. *Lord, you taught us all to forgive as you forgive us. And so I ask you now, if my prayers have any merit, forgive my brother for his terrible deed. He betrayed you with a kiss. How many times did we all betray you, forsake you, abandon you when we were faced with temptation or suffering for your sake?*

Matthias' ears were now ringing endlessly. A huge stone had cracked his skull and blood poured in rivulets from the wound. Everything began to fade away. One thing alone came into focus amidst the mounting fog. A man was approaching. Somehow he was ignored by the mob, peacefully weaving around the others unnoticed. He stopped by Matthias' side and crouched down a few inches from him. Matthias summoned the very last of his energy to gaze up at the man. The Lord! *At last, the time has come… he has returned for me, just as he promised!* His Divine Friend stooped down and placed his head alongside Matthias'. The old man pressed his dying lips to the Lord's cheek and spoke the words, "Hail, Rabbouni!" Judas' kiss and words of betrayal now baptized with his successor's faithful tears, Matthias closed his eyes one last time.

CHAPTER ELEVEN

Simon & Jude

J ude felt disoriented in the scorching heat. The arid atmosphere brought out a steady flow of perspiration that mingled with the blood that seeped from his many wounds. He had neither eaten nor tasted a drop of water in days, and the hunger and thirst weighed heavily on him.

"Jude?" whispered a familiar voice not far away.

"Simon! Praise God, you're still alive!" Jude managed despite his condition.

Simon was in the next cell. He was in similar condition, beset by hunger, thirst, and wracked with the painful effects of the guards' handiwork. Simon sat in the only corner from which he could see the beautiful, purplish blue sky through an almost imperceptible crack in the mud brick ceiling. Gazing out in even such limited measure brought Simon a small but significant sense of peace. The One who painted that sky was waiting for him and his fellow prisoner.

"Jude," Simon said, quite softly. "Do you remember the day he called us?"

"Of course, brother," Jude replied as the consoling warmth of the memory enfolded him.

The rolling hills of Galilee spread out all around them and there, on a high hilltop above, stood the Lord. Word of this mysterious man had preceded him, and before long the crowds gathered from near and far to hear what he had to say. Jude was by no means a stranger to the Lord, for they were cousins. Some had been surprised when the carpenter had begun preaching in public and even performing miracles, but Jude had not. From their childhood he and his brother James had known there was something special about their kin. He had a presence that seemed to fill your soul with life and peace. Somehow, Jude always felt more alive, more fully himself when he was near his cousin. The doubts and fears fell away like leaves and you were left with a sense of clarity, simplicity, resolve.

Commotion outside their crude cell doors startled the musing pair. Bloodthirsty voices echoed in the corridor and Jude and Simon could not help but overhear every word.

"They will pay! They will pay by sunset for their sorcery!" shouted one man.

Simon recognized the voice. He had been their chief accuser, the priest and adviser to the Persian army commander. When he learned of these foreigners' presence in their lands before a great battle, he assured his master that the gods' silence was a result of the apostles' magic. The commander had questioned them and Simon and Jude assured him that there would be no battle at all; the following day would see the enemy army sue for

peace. When it happened just as they had said, Simon and Jude were praised and honored, and the Persian holy man sought their blood over the humiliation.

"Bring them now! There's no point in delaying any further," another voice agreed with an air of urgent vengeance.

Simon felt fear begin to swell within. He closed his eyes slowly and tightly, seeking to rekindle the memory once more. It did not take long. He stood in a vast crowd listening with attentive curiosity to the carpenter's son, this man so wise and mysterious yet familiar and approachable. Simon had been a Zealot, very proud indeed of his deeply rooted patriotism. He yearned to be like the great heroes of Israel: Samson and David and Judas Maccabeus. He had dreamed of the arrival of the Messiah, the one who would gather the twelve tribes once more and do battle with Israel's enemies.

Then that moment had arrived. The memory was still difficult to believe for both Simon and Jude. The Lord had called them, singled them out, given them and the other ten the power they could still not begin to comprehend or merit for themselves. Simon could not miss the significance of their number. Twelve gathered to do battle, but not with other men, other sinners in desperate need of the Lord's loving grace. No. They were to battle against evil and death itself. Every day that had passed since that day brought Simon more assurance that God

had answered his youthful prayers more profoundly than he could ever have imagined.

Jude, for his part, grew to love the cousin who had fixed him so firmly in wonder and awe ever more deeply. And after he had risen from the dead, Jude never lived a single day but at the Lord's side. Fear had vanished years ago. Though he knew this day was to be the last in this life for him and his friend, he was at peace and he began to pray intently for the men who were about to do such terrible deeds. Some would call them hopeless cases. Jude would never give up on them.

The doors flew open and crashed against the wall. Small bits of mud brick shook loose and fell from the walls and ceiling. Frenzied guards rushed in upon both men and took hold of them, riotously rushing them forth from the prison into the hot evening air. It was nearly sunset. In the distance Simon could see a roughly built wooden table near the soldiers' camp. There were menacing guards gathering there, clearing it off and motioning for him to be brought to them.

Jude meanwhile was led to an ancient looking marble pillar about his height and stained a reddish-brown hue from untold amounts of spilt blood. He looked toward Simon and their eyes met. Simon's were marked by tears of a fear that was real, yet passing.

"I will see you in a few moments, brother!" Jude cried out to him. Simon nodded, his clenched jaw trembling ever so slightly.

The guards struck Jude in the face with a knotted wooden club. He was dazed, vision blurred, and he could not hear out of his right ear. Blood raced from fresh wounds and he tried to look for Simon once more. He could not see him; in fact, he could not seem to see anything except the most extraordinary sight he had ever seen.

Meanwhile, not far away, Simon was thrown onto the table before he knew what happened. Guards strapped him down so tightly that he quickly lost feeling in his legs and feet and it was very difficult to breathe. The executioners were laughing and shouting obscenities as they scurried about, rifling through various weapons and instruments of torture. He could not mistake the wicked satisfaction on their faces and in their voices when they agreed upon the saw. Fear, panic, horror should have conquered him, but something else did instead. Simon could see what Jude was seeing.

The Lord was here! He stood a short distance away. A soothing, peaceful light poured forth from him in every direction. Simon and Jude drank in the sight like water, though everyone else was blind to the Lord and his glory. Guards near Jude readied arrows on their tense bowstrings and they took aim at the pillar-bound apostle. He did not even look at them.

Simon's executioners began their dreadful work with vim and vigor. Yet as he faded from consciousness, he fixed his last ounce of attention on the Lord's face. It was wet with tears of sorrow and

infinitely greater rejoicing. This was no end of life, it was the beginning.

Arrows burst forth from their bows and riddled Jude in a flash of white-hot pain followed by a cold, emptying sensation. As his life poured out upon the dusty ground, Jude looked at that same face. The world grew dim, but Jude smiled one last time as the Light of the World took its place forever

CHAPTER TWELVE

John

*T*he beloved disciple, he thought with an amused grin. *That's what he always called me! Why me? Why am I still here?* John's mind marveled at such mysteries frequently. He stood today at the mouth of a cave overlooking the rocky coastline near Ephesus. He had been the bishop here for many years, but ever since his recent return from exile on Patmos, he preferred to pray, work, and sleep in the cave by the sea. He had seen incredible things on that island. The Lord had shown him ineffable visions, and he pondered them every day now.

The words he had written by the Lord's will were to be his last, he knew it in his heart. He could never write again after writing such things. All mystery was already there, hidden in plain sight now for all generations to hear, to read, to unpack by the guidance of the Lord's Spirit and his Church.

Why am I still here? He pondered the question again. *The others are long since with you, Lord. And yet I am here, an old man, frail and crumbling.* He thought about his many years. *How young was I when he called James and me? Sixteen? Seventeen?* He couldn't quite remember. His mind was slower these days. It took him so long sometimes to remember things. Names

of his flock were difficult to recall. He lost his place when speaking to others far more now than he once had. Occasionally he would discover that he was repeating himself, but his beloved children in the Lord were always so kind to him that they never pointed it out. By God's grace though he never forgot a single detail about the Lord himself. That was all clearer to him now than ever before, and whenever he thought he could not love the Lord more, he had been proven wrong.

John winced from acute pain in his knees that had grown increasingly familiar. He had to sit. He gripped a small nearby tree branch tightly as he waited for the pain to subside. Trying to think about something else, he looked down at his feet. They were mangled, calloused, wrinkled and covered with scars. *How many roads have you tread, old friends?* He laughed a little, then winced again as another aching twinge made its unwelcome visit. John pressed the thought further. Aged feet, weary and nearly broken knees, legs wasting away, withered arms that could no longer carry any significant weight. He remembered what it felt like to run as a boy and how he had grown strong and vigorous. Peter tried to keep up with him as they ran to the empty tomb, but he didn't stand a chance in those days! John smiled again at the memory. Those were days when he could stand his ground even as the storm battered their fishing boat on the raging sea.

John looked at his hands. They ached constantly now, even when he was not using them. *No more*

fishing... no more mending nets. He curled and bent his fingers a little and tried to make a fist. It wasn't easy. *Are these the same hands, Lord? The same hands that shook you awake in the boat when we lost faith? Are these the same hands that held the cup of wine that had once been water and the cup of your precious blood that had once been wine? The hands that distributed the bread that had once been scarce and your glorious body that had once been bread? Are these the hands that took you down from the Cross? The hands your Holy Spirit guided to write so many words to your beloved flock?* He looked at how weak and unusable they had now become. *I'll never write again*, he lamented.

It was almost dawn. He loved to get out here early before anyone else was even awake. It made him feel a sense of youth that nothing else could produce any longer. He tried to stand up, but it was no use. *No worry*, he thought, *someone will be along later.* His mind wandered once more before arriving at a subject that always made him both blissful and sad. *The others. O my friends, my brothers! How I miss you! How many more years have I spent apart from you than in your company!* John knew they were always with him, but he longed to see them, to embrace them again, to hear their voices. He longed to hear Philip's laugh and to hear Andrew's stories and to go fishing with his brother James.

John had heard of each one of their terrible deaths over the seventy years since they all walked with the Lord. He mourned each of them in turn, praising God for their courageous witness and

weeping oceans of tears over their absence on the earth. *It is better for you to be with the Lord, praying for us and inspiring us*, he would always say when he thought of them. *But I do miss you*, he could not help but add. John had also struggled with a sense of guilt. *Why them? Why not me? Lord, may I be truly about your work! If you call me to die for you like my brothers did, you know Lord that I will!*

His chest was starting to hurt now. John rubbed it but the pain kept coming in ever greater surges. His left arm was tightening and it hurt as well. He shook it a bit and rubbed it. Glancing once more to the coast, John blinked his eyes several times. What he first mistook for fog or haze he soon realized was his own vision growing blurry. The burning in his chest was mounting as well and it became more difficult to breathe. John blinked again, shook his head and decided to lie down on the smooth rock beside where he had been sitting. After a few minutes, he felt dizzy. He prayed more intently. *Lord... Lord forgive me! Forgive my weakness, my selfishness in this late hour. I am yours forever, Lord! When it is time, receive my spirit, Lord! Come, Lord Jesus!*

John was fading. His heart grew weaker with each beat and he could feel his old, beaten, burnt-out body shutting down. Hazy eyes darted around taking in their final sights. As they did, John beheld an astonishing thing. Not far off the coast, a boat came into view. It was a small fishing vessel, emerging out of the dawn mist as though out of a

dream. It settled on the shore not thirty yards from where the apostle lay, and several people began to disembark. At first, John could not recognize any of them. But then one of them shouted with a voice he could never have mistaken.

"What are you lying around for?! Mother always said you were lazier than me!"

"James!" John managed.

Now he could see the men getting off the boat as clear as the breaking day. *My brothers!* They were all there, waving and calling to him with hearty excitement and bidding him to join them on the boat. James, his brother. Philip and Matthew. Peter and Paul and Andrew. Nathanael, Thomas, James, Matthias, Simon, and Jude. The others had returned for him, and they were not alone.

Last of all, the Lord Jesus came forth, passing through their midst and kneeling by John's side. The old man wept with joy as he reached up for his beloved friend. Then, placing his head upon John's chest, the Lord spoke.

"Well done, my good and faithful servant. Now, enter into my joy!"

EPILOGUE

The radiant sun began to take its leave for the day, sinking down on the other side of the old city. The blistering heat of that day slowly retreated and was replaced by a cool and sweet evening air. People scuttled about in the street outside her window as she lay in her bed and her heart warmed at the thought of them, whoever they were.

Mary was not alone. Her sons and her daughters, for that is what they had become to her, came to her bedside every so often. She assured them she was fine, just resting, and asked them to sit with her for a while. They were more than happy to oblige. She was mother to them all, the woman whose faith had been the doorway through which heaven had come to earth. Boundless did her love for all God's children seem, and that was why they had all become her children as well. She loved each person with the very love of her Divine Son.

One face she had been waiting for appeared in the doorway and her eyes, filled with the light of all ages, brightened with joy.

"John," she said softly.

The beloved disciple of her son moved swiftly to her side and took her hand in his.

"Mother. What is it?" he asked her.

"Did I ever tell you about the time, many years ago now, when he went missing?"

"Went missing? Where?" he replied.

"During the Passover, when we were all journeying back to Nazareth," she said with a wry grin.

"No! You never told me this story," John said with piqued interest.

Mary continued.

"Joseph thought he was with me, and I thought he was with him. It took us three days to find him, and do you know where he was the whole time?"

John shrugged. He had leaned close to her in rapt attention and curiosity.

"The Temple!" she laughed and gazed her love-filled eyes into his. "Joseph and I were so worried about him. We told him so when we found him there. The whole scene was astounding. He was with the learned men of the Temple, asking them questions and teaching them as well. I had never seen such a thing."

John shook his head in amazement. The Lord had never told him this story. It should have come as no surprise, for whenever he thought he could not love the Lord more, he had been proven wrong.

"What did he say?" John pressed closer. Mary smiled at him and reached up a withered hand to caress his face. Though the years had begun to turn

his hair gray, he posed the question like an eager child.

"He was so calm. We couldn't help but be put at ease straight away. Then he simply said, 'Why were you searching for me? Did you not know that I must be about my Father's work?'"

John smiled broadly and nodded. *Of course he said that*, he thought. That was the Lord. John was not surprised in the least that his beloved friend had, even in his youth, been so captivating. *Lord*, he whispered in his heart while tightening his loving grip on Mary's precious hand, *you are as you said, the Way, the Truth, and the Life.*

Mary closed her eyes and prayed silently as well. Her prayer arose to the throne of the Lord, a prayer of extraordinary beauty and power. She had always been his, "the handmaiden of the Lord" as she had exclaimed so long ago at the angel's message. She kept her eyes shut and remembered it all, those moments she had pondered and treasured in her heart. The sensation of knowing that he grew within her womb. How her heart alighted with exuberance the first time she felt him move and kick and turn. She remembered her joy at his miraculous birth in the first cave and her intolerable anguish at his burial in the second.

Finally, she remembered how it felt to see him in his full glory after yet another three days of bleakest darkness without him. He had approached her so very tenderly, as only a son can. She wept tears of utter bliss that day. He reached up to her,

cupping her face in his strong yet wounded hands. Those hands had once gripped her finger in loving trust. They had fashioned gifts for her and wrapped round her affectionately. They had healed the sick and even raised the dead. He had ultimately allowed them to be destroyed in order to reach this moment, the moment from hence all men would come to know the Good News - that he was risen!

She grew tired. John sat quietly with her, the son her own Son had given to her when his hour had come. Mary loved John so, this apostle who had taken her into his care some twenty years ago. She felt as though she was beginning to fall asleep. It seemed closer at each moment as she passed into that secret place between one's consciousness and the dawning of a dream.

Presently she saw what appeared to be light approaching through the darkness. It began as a small glimmer, very far off. Soon she could see that it was brighter than the sun, but her eyes were not harmed by staring into it. In fact, as she did she felt stronger, more energetic, more alive. The light was getting closer and closer. Now only a few yards away from her, she could see clearly and fully. *My Son!* She fell to her knees before him and he rushed to pick her up.

"Mother," he said in that voice. The Voice.

"O, my Son!" Mary cried out with the voice of her now consummated life.

"I've come back for you," he whispered in her ear.

The King of Kings kissed her cheek, and the Queen Mother fell into a sleep that brought her into eternity.

ACKNOWLEDGEMENTS

Human beings are fundamentally social creatures, so it should come as no surprise that our creative efforts, though deeply personal and individual experiences, are nonetheless influenced and shaped by an astonishing network of others. This book has its roots in the most intimate depths of my soul, yet it could never have arrived in your hands without the support and guidance of people I truly believe God himself drew into this project. I must begin by asking forgiveness for anyone whom I fail to mention or whose role in all this is still known only to God, but here are at least a few folks I need to thank:

My parents and grandparents, for nourishing my every creative aspiration from the earliest age

My brother Joe and all of the seminarians and priests to whom I dedicate this book, for their early and regular encouragement of this project and their insistence that I publish it

<u>Every English teacher I've ever had</u>, for helping me to write well, not just good

<u>Steve Ray</u>, for his gracious review of the book which appears on the cover, and for guiding our pilgrimage group through the Holy Land in 2009 (so much grace came from that pilgrimage!)

<u>Joseph Pearce</u>, whose kind, encouraging words about this endeavor took me by surprise and filled me with previously unreached levels of confidence

<u>Kathy Roe</u>, whose artistic eye can make even me look presentable in an "About the Author" photo!

<u>The countless people who pray for me each day</u>, for giving me wings to flee the enemy

Finally, <u>my wife Kristine and my little girls Noelle and Renata</u>, without whose love and support I know I would not be half the man I am today.

APOSTLES' FEAST DAYS

Catholic Liturgical Calendar

May 3 - Feast of Saints Philip & James the Lesser

May 14 - Feast of Saint Matthias

June 29 - Feast of Saints Peter & Paul

July 3 - Feast of Saint Thomas

July 25 - Feast of Saint James the Greater

August 24 - Feast of Saint Bartholomew (Nathanael)

September 21 - Feast of Saint Matthew

October 28 - Feast of Saints Simon & Jude

November 30 - Feast of Saint Andrew

December 27 - Feast of Saint John

ABOUT THE AUTHOR

Michael Creavey

 Mike Creavey holds a master's degree in theology and Christian ministry from Franciscan University of Steubenville. At thegraciousguest.org, he explores the intersection of faith and culture through movies, books, food, music, and much more. Mike lives near Harrisburg, PA with his wife and daughters.